Along Came a Birdie

MORE true crime and real-life stories from a small-town bird reporter

SUSAN TOWHEE

COPYRIGHT

Towhee Tales Publishing, 2024

First edition print ISBN - 9798218281212

Towhee Tales Publishing

Nashville, TN

towheetalespublishing@gmail.com

DISCLAIMER

Any references to real people, real places, characters, company names, or historical events are used fictitiously.

DEDICATION

To my brother, Victor, who can fix anything, just like Vincent Vulture.

To Darren McGavin, whose Kolchak voice I use to sound out Susan's reporting thoughts.

To my cousin, Connie, who told me a long time ago that I should write a book one day.

RESTFUL ROOST MAP

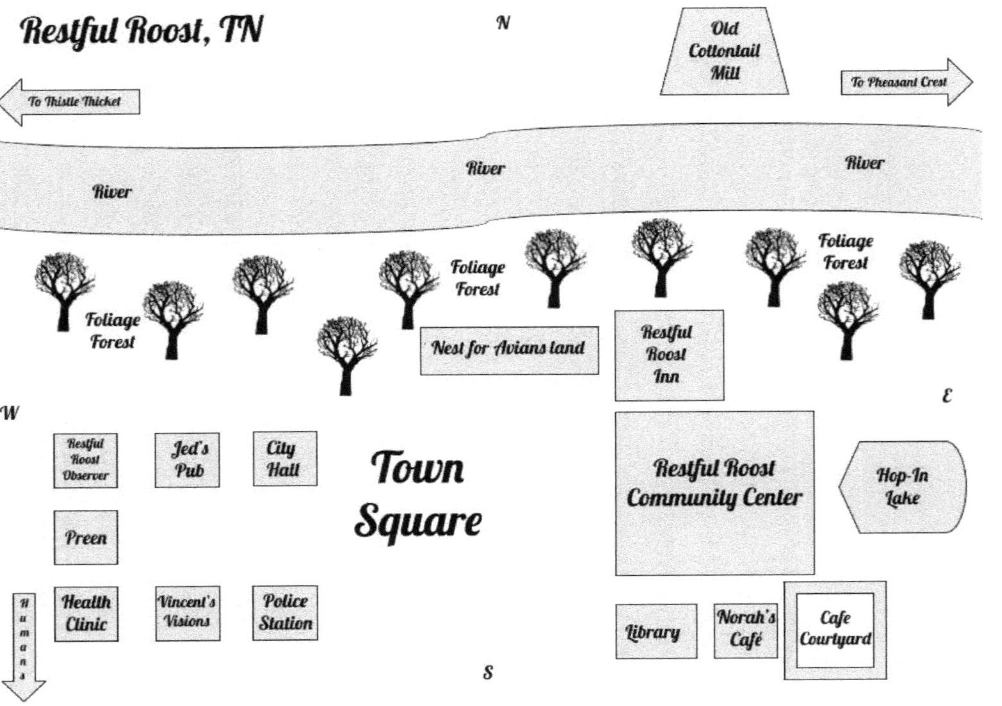

RESTFUL ROOST RESIDENTS

Susan - Eastern Towhee *Pipilo erythrophthalmus*
Adam - Eastern Towhee *Pipilo erythrophthalmus*
Thea - Northern Bobwhite *Colinus virginianus*
Norah - White-breasted Nuthatch *Sitta carolinensis*
Goldy - American Goldfinch *Spinus tristis*
Mary - American Robin *Turdus migratorius*
Charlene - Carolina Chickadee *Poecile carolinensis*
Alex - American Crow *Corvus brachyrhynchos*
Katherine - Great Blue Heron *Ardea herodias*
Tara - Tufted Titmouse *Baeolophus bicolor*
Jed - Pomarine Jaeger *Stercorarius pomarinus*
Peter - Pileated Woodpecker *Dryocopus pileatus*
Abby- Mallard *Anas platyrhynchos*
Millard - Mallard *Anas platyrhynchos*
Hopper - Eastern Cottontail *Sylvilagus floridanus*
Evelyn - Eastern Cottontail *Sylvilagus floridanus*
Simon - Song Sparrow *Melospiza melodia*
Vincent - Black Vulture *Coragyps atratus*
Liza - Black Vulture *Coragyps atratus*
Chad - Northern Cardinal *Cardinalis cardinalis*
Vanessa -House Sparrow *Passer domesticus*
David - Downy Woodpecker *Dryobates pubescens*
Gary - Canada Goose *Branta canadensis*
Restful Roost Rocs Hockey Team - *Canada Geese Branta canadensis*

THE STORIES

INTRODUCTION

The crime wave has died down in Restful Roost, but mayhem still occurs!

What follows in these pages are MORE true crime and real-life stories from Restful Roost.

Join me, a bird reporter for the local newspaper, as I entertain you with tales of birdnapping, a bug infestation, a rare bird sighting, and poisoning!

Welcome to Restful Roost!

~ 1 ~

BLACK CROW MOAN

The Story (as I remember it)...

February 12, 2023

With only two days left until the world-famous Sultry Silkie chicken show at the community center on Valentine's Day, Restful Roost was abuzz with excitement. The chickens perform their titillating dances set to swing music. Tickets had been sold out since the first of the year. My mate, Adam, scored box seats for the show. He also took advantage of the half-off local wine bottle special at the award-winning restaurant in the Restful Roost Inn. I was looking forward to peace and quiet until the big day. I hoped that I could score a back stage pass to the show as I am a reporter with the town's newspaper, the Restful Roost Observer. How little did I know that intense drama would engulf the next two days before Cupid's special day!

My first stop that morning was at the Restful Roost Library for our weekly book club meeting. That week we were discussing the new book in the Sophie Kimball Mysteries by J.C. Eaton. Thea Bobwhite, the town librarian, obtained advance copies for us to read the newest release titled *Strike Out 4 Murder.* Each book is funnier than the last! Also in attendance for the meeting were Norah Nuthatch, Goldy Goldfinch, Mary Robin, Charlene Chickadee, and a new member, Alex Crow.

Me: "Hi ladies! And Alex, so glad to see you have joined us!"

Norah: "Alex, I didn't know you were a book lover!"

Alex: "Hey everybird! Well, no, I don't like reading. I just know this is the juiciest place in town for gossip!"

Thea: "Hold up, you can't be a member if you don't read! I won't allow it!"

Mary: "Oh no, Alex. Now you have done it. Do not upset Thea when it comes to books!"

Alex: "Pleeease let me stay! I promise I will give the next book a try!"

Thea: "I expect a lively group discussion for next week's book!"

Alex: "Next week?! You mean you all read a book each week?"

Goldy: "Uh yes, that is the point of a weekly meeting!

Question is, how much do you desire juicy gossip? If you really are interested, then you will need to participate."

Alex: "Good point. So what is the news in RR this week? You start first Charlene!"

Thea: "Nope. I run this meeting. First off we will discuss the book."

After a quick discussion about the baseball-themed murder in the Kimball book, we then traded news stories and goings-ons. Thea shared that she has a very controversial guest lined up for a book talk in the summer, but she would not give details. Norah, the owner of Norah's Café, mentioned a new seed line that she is trying out at the café. Goldy, the town realtor, discussed new nest listings in the area. Town doctor, Mary Robin, shared that she will be taking an actual vacation soon to Gatlinburg. Charlene, in her role as the events coordinator at the community center, gave an update on the Silkie chicken show. Alex was the owner of the only salon in town, Preen. He shared with us details on a new line of conditioner he just got in. The conversation started dying down after each bird's updates so we started packing up our things. Then Alex chimed in with details on his new client.

Alex: "Well, I need to be flying out. I have a new customer and let me tell you, she is a wingful!"

Mary: "New customer? Do we have a new bird in town?"

Alex: "I guess. She said she just flew in for a visit with friends. She won't give me her name and she always pays in cash. Super sketchy, right? All I know is she is an Indigo

Bunting and has already made four appointments this week. Today she is coming in for a feather dye. I guess she can be as weird as she wants if she is paying me."

Me: "Ha! Be sure to save a spot for me so I can get my feathers done before the Silkie chicken show!"

Alex: "Come by anytime! I will fit you in! Oh, there is another bird in town that I do know the name of! Tara Titmouse! The mayor just hired her to help out at his pub.

Goldy: "I was wondering when Mayor Jed would find help. With all the mayoral duties, he can't run a bar by himself anymore."

Alex: "Mmm-hmm. I stopped in for a nightcap last night. After an hour of dealing with Miss Bunting's nails, I needed a drink! I met Tara and talked to her for quite a while. She and the mayor met at a Cannibal Cormorant concert a few weeks ago in Lousiville. They are into the same crazy metal music, apparently. Tara mentioned to him that she was looking for a new job and maybe a new town. She said he convinced her to give Restful Roost a try and help out at his bar. She could not stop talking about Mayor Jed! If you ask me, she is interested in a lot more than a new town. Wink wink."

Me: "Anybird else want to grab dinner after work at Jed's so we can meet Tara?"

Norah: "Count me in!"

Charlene: "Me, too!"

Alex: "Ladies, I will be there as well. Oh, and Vincent Vulture, is dating Liza Vulture!"

Thea: "Wow, how do you find all this stuff out?"

Alex: "I told you all before, when you offer a free glass

of champagne while you are getting work done at the spa, birds will talk!"

Me: "We should hire you at the paper to write a column!"

Alex: "Oh no! Bird secrets are safe with me!

Goldy: "Hold up, Vincent Vulture was at Preen? How did you deal with the...you know...vulture smell?"

Alex: "Actually, vultures keep themselves pretty clean. Since he has the hots for Liza he wants to get extra work done. I hear wedding bells if you ask me! Gots to fly! Toodles!"

The next stop was work at the Restful Roost Observer. My editor, Katherine Heron, was screaming at somebird on the phone about who knows what. I am sure she had been at the office since 4 a.m. or so. I hid away in my office all day doing various research for stories and perusing the Restful Roost Inn restaurant menu. Did I want a bottle of Beachaven Jazz or Del Monaco Chardonnay with my appetizers? Those decisions would have to be made with my mate, Adam, before Valentine's Day. As soon as 5 p.m. hit, I was out the door and walking to Jed's Pub for dinner. I heard Katherine yelling at another bird (maybe the same one?) again on my way out.

When I arrived at Jed's, Norah and Charlene were

already there and had a spot waiting for me at a table near the bar. I joined them and was excited to hang out and excited to meet Tara. Soon a gorgeous little Tufted Titmouse walked over to our table. This had to be Tara!

Tara: “Hi ladies! My name is Tara. Nice to see all of ya’ll! What would everybird like to drink and eat?”

Me: “I would like an Uncle Nearest bourbon neat. Wait, should we wait to order food until Alex gets here?”

Charlene: “Blue Moon for me! Yes, I can wait until he gets here.”

Norah: “I will take a gin and tonic.”

Tara: “Ok! Coming right up!”

Me: “Hold up! How do you like Restful Roost so far? I am Susan Towhee, by the way. I work at the local paper.”

Tara: “Nice to meet ya! I love it here! Jed was right about how wonderful the town and the people are!”

Charlene: “Jed needed help so it is great you moved here to help him out.”

Tara: “Oh, I would do anything for Jed! Say, here comes Alex. I will get those drinks ready and then come back to get his order.”

Tara scurried off as Alex ran over to us. We didn’t even get a chance to discuss how lovestruck Tara was.

Alex: “Oh my god! Ladies! That bunting is so creepy! She kept talking and wouldn’t let me leave. Then she wanted to book another treatment for tomorrow!

Me: “Well isn’t that a good thing? More business right?”

Alex: "Um, I can sense crazy. And that bird is cray cray."

Norah: "Well, just cancel on her or close the shop."

Alex: "I can't! I am booked solid for V-Day, but she demanded to be seen. I told her she could stop by and I could try to squeeze her in. She said she would be there when the store opened! I might call Chief Mallard and see if he can stop by."

Charlene: "The police chief? Are you that scared of this bird? Aren't buntings tiny little things?"

Alex: "I told you! I know the signs!"

Tara arrived with our drinks and just in time. Alex needed a strong one!

Tara: "Here ya go ladies! Alex, what can I get you?"

Alex: "Bring me a margarita in your largest glass please and ASAP!"

Tara: "You got it!"

Tara scurried away again. She clearly knew when alcohol was needed.

Alex: "Oh, I know! Susan, can you write in the paper tomorrow that I am offering a free feather fluff? That should bring birds in so the place is packed all day and I am not alone with Miss Bunting."

Me: "Sure thing. Did you get her name today?"

Alex: "No! She won't tell me!"

Norah: "OK, that is odd. I haven't even seen her around. Where does she go all day? I mean, besides your salon."

Alex: “Not funny.”

Charlene: “Let’s relax and decide what to eat. What are everybird’s plans for Valentine’s Day?”

Me: “Dinner at the Restful Roost Inn and box seats for the Silkie show!”

Norah: “I guess I will be alone since I am still single.”

Charlene: “Yeah, same for me. Let’s order a pizza and watch horror movies or something.”

Norah: “Deal! Alex, want to join us? You can invite psycho birdie.”

Alex: “Norah...I will slap a bird. But, no, I can’t. I have...plans.”

Charlene: “Plans? With whom?”

Just as Alex was about to share his secret with us we were interrupted by Jed. I had never seen a bird so happy!

Jed: “Hey ladies! And Alex! How are the drinks? What can I get you all to eat tonight?”

Alex: “Oh no, we will get to the food later. Tell us all about Tara.”

Jed blushed and looked at his feet.

Jed: “Isn’t she great? She is helping out a lot around here.”

Alex: “Yeah, I bet she is.”

Jed: “What do you mean?”

Norah: “Jed, it is obvious she likes you. And I just met her!”

Jed: "We are just friends. You know, for now. I mean, I would like to know her better. Do you guys think she will go out with me?"

Me: "Jed. Seriously. Are you that clueless when it comes to females?"

Jed: "I have never really been serious with a lady before."

Alex: "A lady? See, you are smitten. Ask her out ASAP. There are a lot of single birds in this town who will beat you to it. Take her to the Silkie show!"

Norah: "That is sold out!"

Charlene: "Well, I have connections. For a friend, I can help. If she says yes, let me know. I can give you my comp tickets."

Norah: "You have comp tickets? Why aren't we going to that instead of pizza and a movie?"

Charlene: "Girl, I have to get away from that place from time to time."

Norah: "All right, all right. I get it. Ask her Jed! Like, tonight!"

Alex: "Oh! Both of you stop by Preen tomorrow and I will get you a fresh feather clip and Jed, tell Tara I will offer her a feather fluff for free."

Jed: "You will fluff her? What the hell do you mean?"

Me: "Jed, just ask her. We guarantee you she will say yes."

Jed: "OK, but if this goes wrong you all are banned from this pub."

Jed walked away and hopefully was on his way to talk to Tara. We also forgot to order food.

Me: "OK, now who do you have plans with, Alex?"

Before he could answer we heard a loud peter-peter-peter call from the back of the bar. It was clearly a Tufted Titmouse song. A happy titmouse!

Norah: "Well, I guess Jed got his answer!"

Jed ran out and offered a free round for everybird and free mealworm appetizers for all tables. In all the excitement we forgot about Alex's secret date.

SULTRY SILKIE CHICKEN SHOW SOLD OUT

RESTFUL ROOST INN OFFERS WINE SPECIAL

PREEN OFFERING FREE FEATHER FLUFF

by Susan Towhee
Published February 13, 2023 in the Restful Roost Observer

If you planned on seeing the world-famous dancing Silkie Chicken show this February then you are out of luck! "Tickets have been gone since the beginning of the year," Restful Roost Community Center Events Coordinator Charlene Chickadee said. "Their extravagant feathers, smooth dance moves, all accompanied by swing music, have been selling out shows all over the country."

The chicken show is this Valentine's Day, February 14th, at the Restful Roost Community Center at 7 p.m.

Peter Woodpecker, owner of the Restful Roost Inn, is offering half-price bottles of wine either pre-show or post-show at the new restaurant in the inn. "Treat your special loved one, or yourself, to a half-priced bottle of wine," said Woodpecker. "If you are attending the show or not, we would love to see you." The restaurant is located at the inn directly beside the community center.

Need to spruce up before the big day? Head to the local salon, Preen, where you can get a free feather fluff courtesy of owner Alex Crow. "Birds should treat themselves! Stop by for a feather fluff. Male or female, single or taken, come pamper yourself at Preen," said Crow. "We open at 9 a.m. and will stay open until 6 tonight."

Love one another, Restful Roost!

After filing my story at the office, I spent time researching the bizarre 1868 train accident in Restful Roost. I was writing a story on the incident and the crazy aftermath. If you want to know more on that just check out my first book! I then headed to Preen for my feather fluff after lunch. That place was packed! I only said a quick hello to Alex as he worked on my feathers and left so he could move on to the next customer. I looked around to see if I could locate the mysterious bunting, but I couldn't find her anywhere. I then headed home after work to pick out a nice outfit to wear for tomorrow.

A peaceful night was not in the works as around 9 p.m. my mate and I heard a loud cawing outside.

"Hello! Caw! Let me in!" It was Alex!

Me: "What are you screeching about at this time of night?"

Alex: "Girl! That bunting is insane! She was waiting for me when I closed the store and demanded we go out tomorrow night. I told her I just was not interested and she started screaming at me! I flew away only after some very clever evasive maneuvers to lose her."

Me: "So you flew here? Thanks for steering the crazy to my nest!"

Alex: "I am sorry! I didn't know where else to go."

At that point, my mate joined us.

Adam: "I overheard everything. Alex, you must go to the police and file a report."

Alex: "I think you might be right. Tonight I just need a public place to stay. In the morning I will fly over. No need to wake up Chief Mallard tonight. Can you two fly with me to the inn?"

Me: "Good idea! Plenty of birds there."

Adam: "Let's fly."

When we arrived at the Restful Roost Inn owner Peter Woodpecker met us at the door. He and Alex immediately embraced. Adam and I looked at each other and smiled.

Me: "So this is your secret lover?"

Alex: "Yes! We were planning on going public tomorrow so can you keep a secret?"

Me: "Of course we can!"

Adam: "Love is in the air! Isn't it sweet?"

Peter: "Did that crazy bunting do something? She has to leave you alone, Alex!"

Alex: "Yes, she stalked me after work and demanded a date! In the morning I will fly to the police station and let the chief know what is up. Right now I just want a nice hot bath and a glass of wine."

Peter: "I will get a room ready. Susan and Adam, I will

see you both tomorrow. I will save a booth by the fountain just for you two."

Me: "Thanks, Peter! We are excited!"

Adam and I said our goodbyes to Peter and Alex and flew home. I needed a bourbon to settle my nerves before I went to sleep. However, a good night's sleep was not to be had. It was midnight and the police scanner awoke with AST, BRK and BNAP calls at the Restful Roost Inn. Those stood for assault, break-in, and birdnapping! I was worried this was related to Alex so I rushed out the door and flew back to the inn.

Back at the inn, I found Peter Woodpecker and Police Chief Millard Mallard talking. The inn staff surrounded Peter to provide comfort. I didn't see Alex anywhere.

Me: "Chief! Is Alex missing? What happened?"

Chief Mallard: "Yep, it appears so. Peter, can you repeat what happened again so I can fill in my notes a bit more?"

Peter: "Yes. I had just arrived to check if Alex needed anything before going to sleep and I heard a commotion behind me. That crazy bunting that had been harassing Alex was behind me. She must have followed me from the lobby. She knocked me in the head and stole my keys. She let herself into Alex's room and must have taken him away. Our cameras only caught her and him leaving through a back door. They went off in the Foliage Forest."

Chief Mallard: "What do you mean she had been harassing Alex?"

Me: "Alex was going to report it in the morning, chief. Seems like today he had had enough."

Chief Mallard: "Damn, I wish he had talked to me as soon as it happened. Who is this bunting anyway?"

Peter: "She never told him her name. Always paid in cash. I don't think anybird else had even seen her before."

Me: "Should we start a search party to look for Alex?"

Chief Mallard: "Yes, because this bunting is violent. I will go to the station and see if there are any open cases on a female bunting and then alert the mayor. The search party should meet at the town square in an hour!"

With that, the chief flew off. I hugged Peter and told him it would be all right. We would find Alex in time for everybird to have a happy Valentine's Day.

An hour later it seemed like the entire town had shown up to search for Alex. Peter and I had flown around town waking birds up with the call to meet at the town square.

Chief Mallard: "All right! Listen up! Alex Crow has been birdnapped. We know the birdnapper headed into the Foliage Forest, so let's start there and scan the entire area. We need birds on the ground and in the air. Let's meet back here in two hours and report on our findings. Then, we can decide where to look next. The bidnapper is described as a female Indigo Bunting. I have photos printed out from the inn's security camera, so please take one."

Every bird grabbed a printout and flew off to the forest.

Adam and I teamed up with Chief Mallard to search the river's edge. We assumed they wouldn't fly away as Alex, being a large crow and much bigger than a bunting, would be able to quickly get away from the bunting. The bunting must have a weapon trained on him to keep in by her side. Hiding near fresh water might be where they were. As we were searching we heard quacking and rustling near the shore.

Chief Mallard: "Halt! What bird goes there? Identify yourself."

A pretty female mallard appeared from the weeds on the shore and waddled to us. I looked at the chief and he was smitten.

Chief Mallard: "Oh, uh, hello there. Sorry to bother you. We are searching for an American Crow and an Indigo Bunting. Have you seen either of those around here?"

Female Mallard: "Hello, sir. No, I have not seen any birds lately. I just floated up the river from Thistle Thicket. I am a traveling quiltmaker and stopped here for the night. My name is Abby Mallard. I am happy to help you all search for your friends."

Chief Mallard: "Yes, we would appreciate that. Yes, very much so. Thank you. My name is Millard."

Abby: "Nice to meet you, Millard."

Me: "Chief, why don't you and Abby search the river's edge? Ya'll are much better swimmers than me and Adam. We will take flight and search from above."

Chief Mallard: "Good plan Susan. Thanks! Keep me posted if you find anything."

With that, Adam and I flew off. The love sparks were flying and we didn't want to interrupt.

The entire wooded area was searched, but no sign of Alex or the bunting. Back at the town square, the residents met again. We were tired but wired. Chief Mallard told the crowd to go home and get a few hours of sleep. We would meet again in the morning to scan the rest of the town. Instead of going home, I went to the office to file the story for tomorrow.

LOCAL RESIDENT ALEX CROW BIRDNAPPED

UNKNOWN INDIGO BUNTING AT LARGE

RESTFUL ROOST INN OWNER ASSAULTED

TOWN SEARCH PLANNED

by Susan Towhee
Published February 14, 2023 in the Restful Roost Observer

Resident and business owner Alex Crow was birdnapped last night at the Restful Roost Inn. Crow was renting a room at the inn to escape harassment from an unknown female Indigo Bunting that had frequented Preen, Alex's salon, over the past few days.

Owner of the inn, Peter Woodpecker, said he was followed and assaulted by the bunting as he was about to check on Alex in his room. “She came from behind me and hit me on the head,” stated Woodpecker. “When I woke up I found the room messed up and Alex gone.”

Police Chief Millard Mallard called for a search of the Foliage Forest last night, but the search party found nothing. “We scanned the entire forest because that was the direction the two were seen heading to. Unfortunately, nothing was found so we need the citizens to help today to scan the entire town," said Chief Mallard. "We will find Alex and bring the criminal bunting to jail."

Restful Roost residents are encouraged to meet at the town square at 9 a.m. today to fan out and search again. If anybird has any tips for the Restful Roost police please call 55-TWEET.

Stay observant Restful Roost!

At 9 a.m. it seemed like the entire town had shown up again at the town square to search for Alex. The plan this time was to search all town buildings and residences. The police chief asked if I could fly to the Old Cottontail Mill across the river to alert Alex's friend Evelyn Cottontail that Alex was missing and to see if she could help. The Cottontails were Restful Roost's wealthiest family. Patriarch Hopper Cottontail is a big-time Hollywood actor whose family ran and operated the mill for over 200 years. In case you couldn't tell by the name, they are a family of rabbits. Evelyn had helped out on a previous case by using her tracking skills.

Upon arrival at the mill, I saw Evelyn and her grandfather, Hopper Cottontail, sipping coffee at the front door.

Hopper: "Well hello there Miss Towhee. How are you?"

Me: “Not so good Mr. Cottontail. We have a bird missing and I need Evelyn’s help.”

Hopper: “Oh no! Which bird is missing?”

Me: “It’s Alex Crow. He was birdnapped by a bunting last night.”

Evelyn: “Oh no, that same bird that won’t leave him alone?”

Me: “Yes, that is the one. Can you help me track him down? We searched the forest last night but found nothing.”

Evelyn: “Of course. Hop on my back and I will run to the bridge so we can cross the river and get started. Let’s stop by Preen so I can get a sniff of Alex’s scent so I can track him better. See ya grandad!”

With a quick goodbye to Hopper, we were off!

Evelyn made record time to Preen. She found Alex’s closet and sniffed around.

Evelyn: “OK, I have the scent. But, wait.”

Me: “Is there a problem?”

Evelyn: “I think he is here.”

Me: “Here? Where?”

Evelyn: “Does this place have a basement?”

Me: “I have no idea. Alex has never mentioned it.”

We threw back the throw rug and scratched and dug at the floor until we found a trap door.

Evelyn: "He is under there. I am going in. Go fly and find the chief."

Me: "Wait! What if you need help?"

Evelyn: "I can take the bunting. Go get reinforcements!"

I flew off and called for help the entire time. Soon enough a large crowd (that included the police chief) were flying back with me to Preen.

Back at Preen we found Evelyn with a bird in her mouth (not dead, just stunned) waiting outside. We also heard lots of yelling and screaming from Alex.

Alex: "You nut job! Did you think you could get away with this? This is like a Lifetime movie! What a psycho!"

Chief Mallard: "OK, let's have some order. I will take this bird away soon. Thank you Miss Evelyn for your assistance. Everybird else, thank you for your help as well. We are all relieved this was resolved in time for a very happy Valentine's Day."

Alex: "Thank you all so much for being there for me! I have the best friends ever!"

The chief turned and smiled at Abby Mallard who was in the crowd. Everybird clapped and praised Evelyn for saving the day. Alex cried and nestled her fur. Simon Sparrow, the town nurse, flew over to check Alex out for injuries. Chief Mallard got Evelyn's statement and took the bunting into custody and to the police station. What a day!

The Restful Roost Inn restaurant was packed to capacity for dinner that night. I sat with Adam on a cute bench with a wonderful view of the fountain outside. We decided on the Beachaven wine, by the way.

Also in the dining room were Vincent Vulture and Liza Vulture, Millard Mallard and Abby Mallard, Mayor Jed Jaeger and Tara Titmouse, and Alex Crow and Peter Woodpecker. Over at the bar, we spotted local architect in training Chad Cardinal with my cousin Vanessa Sparrow. Good for her for finding a bird with an actual job! She did not have a good track record in finding good mates.

After a delicious dinner, we walked across the street to see the Silkie Chicken Show. The chickens did not disappoint!

ALEX CROW FOUND

BIRDNAPPER TAKEN INTO CUSTODY

SULTRY SILKIE CHICKEN SHOW ENTERTAINS

by Susan Towhee
Published February 15, 2023 in the Restful Roost Observer

Recent birdnapping victim Alex Crow was found safe yesterday morning. He was taken by an Indigo Bunting identified as Betty Bunting by Police Chief Millard Mallard. "The bunting named Betty was wanted in New Jersey for a similar crime. She was suffering from nymphomania and claims she could not help her attraction to Mr. Crow," stated Chief Mallard. "She will be sent to the Portland Home for Quirky Birds for rehabilitation."

Thanks to the help of resident Evelyn Cottontail, Alex was found in the basement of his salon, Preen. "I was able to sniff him out. I saw the bunting had a gun on him so I quickly held her down and disarmed her so Alex could get away," said Cottontail. "Then I waited until law enforcement came to take her away."

Mayor Jed Jaeger praised Evelyn and the police in his statement: "I guess crime is still happening, but we have a competent chief now who can put a plan together. We are grateful for Chief Mallard and for Evelyn Cottontail. Restful Roost is proud to call you both residents."

The sold-out Sultry Silkie Chicken show was a huge success. The choreographer for the chickens, Madame Henhooper, was impressed with the Restful Roost Community Center and the amenities it offered. "My chickens received great care here. The staff at the center was able to rush ship a special type of dust that we use for cleaning our feathers," said Henhooper.

Residents are already hoping for another show soon. "Those chickens had such beautiful feathers and colors," said resident Liza Vulture. "I hope they make another visit soon so we can see more of their talents."

Stay safe Restful Roost!

Just another day in Restful Roost!

~ 2 ~

THE APHID AFFLICTION

The Story (as I remember it)...

March 26th, 2023

Love was in the air last month and those cupid arrows that were shot meant nests were being built and baby birds were about to be created. For me, I took up gardening and I am happy to say that I had a nice patch of sunflower seeds planted. Nothing like eating what you grow with your own wings!

The go-to event at the Restful Roost Community Center that March was the first annual home and garden show. Community Center Events Coordinator Charlene Chickadee was able to get world-renowned home and garden and DIY expert Irene Sandpiper as a guest speaker. Irene is a mega star in the bird world! She has her own line of garden tools, cookbooks, and seeds. Plus she has a global

TV network. Local businessbird and architect Vincent Vulture was in charge of the setup and booth displays for the event. The show was set for March 28-29 so the town had a couple of days left to prepare. I headed over to the community center to get the deets on the show.

When I arrived at the community center I found Charlene and Vincent busy working.

Me: "Hello friends! What are you birds working on?"

Vincent: "Just making sure everything is perfect for the show, Susan!"

Charlene: "I don't know how Vincent has the energy to do what he does!"

Vincent: "Well, I have a bit of extra motivation. I asked Liza to marry me at the Silkie Chicken show. The wedding will be the final night of the garden show at the orchid display."

Me: "Oh my, Vincent! That is so wonderful! Congrats!"

Vincent: "Thank you! The orchids in the background will make for great wedding photos!"

Charlene: "I sure hope we have no surprises at the show. Irene demands perfection and I want her to see that Restful Roost was the perfect choice for this event. How about we take a break and grab lunch at Jed's?"

We all agreed and flew off to Jed's Pub for a tasty lunch.

While at Jed's I said a quick hello to Jed's new helper, Tara Titmouse. Jed Jaeger, pub owner, and town mayor, waved from the bar. Charlene provided more details on the show as Tara walked to our booth to take our order.

Charlene: "So I had a visit from the Pheasant Crest Community Center Events Coordinator Shelly Waxwing yesterday. She accused me of stealing Irene Sandpiper's time for our garden show."

Vincent: "Stealing? Irene chose to be the guest speaker here."

Charlene: "Yes, I know! Shelly said Restful Roost wasn't sophisticated enough to hold a home and garden show and Irene would be better off speaking to the birds in Pheasant Crest."

Tara: "That sounds uppity to me!"

Me: "Tara, people over in Pheasant Crest think very highly of themselves."

Tara: "So I have heard!"

Vincent: "Irene knows where to spend her time wisely and she chose Restful Roost for a reason."

Charlene: "Yes, Irene told me she liked our facilities better than other towns she toured. Anyway, let's eat! Tara, I want a fully loaded worm sandwich and water."

Vincent: "Anything Jed is about to throw away will be fine with me."

Me: "I will take a worm sandwich with mustard and water as well. Gotta stay hydrated out there!"

Tara: "You got it! Coming right up!"

After lunch, I headed back to the office to submit the story on the show. My boss, Katherine Heron, was busy at work in her office with the door closed. I don't think she ever leaves that room! Once work was complete I flew home to tend to my sunflower patch and prepare dinner with my mate, Adam.

FIRST ANNUAL HOME & GARDEN SHOW

IRENE SANDPIPER FEATURED SPEAKER

RARE ORCHIDS ON DISPLAY

VULTURE WEDDING DATE SET

by Susan Towhee
Published March 27, 2023 in the Restful Roost Observer

Restful Roost will have its first home and garden show at the Restful Roost Community Center on March 28th and 29th. Guest speakers will include local businessbird Vincent Vulture and world-famous television personality Irene Sandpiper. Food trucks and various booths will be on-site as well. A rare orchid display will also be set up. Look for the full lineup in tomorrow's Observer.

"Irene Sandpiper will discuss proper nesting techniques specific to birds and she will provide a talk on orchid care," Restful Roost Community Center Events Coordinator Charlene Chickadee said. "She will also sign copies of her new book, *Roosting with Irene*."

Tickets are $5.00 for a single-day entry and $8.00 for a two-day ticket.

Vincent Vulture announced his wedding with Liza Vulture will be on the last day of the show at the orchid display. Restful Roost residents are encouraged to attend the wedding. No charge for this portion of the event!

Get excited Restful Roost!

The next morning I headed over to the town library to research the 1868 train explosion incident. Check out my last book for details on that! What a story! Since I was already at the library I stayed for the weekly book club meeting. All the usual suspects (Thea Bobwhite,

Goldy Goldfinch, Mary Robin, Norah Nuthatch, and Alex Crow) were there except for Charlene, who was busy at the community center. The book to discuss that day was, of course, Irene's new one, *Roosting with Irene.* Our town librarian, Thea, always had the newest releases.

Me: "Hey ladies! Everyone excited for the home and garden show?"

Goldy: "You know it! I can't wait for the nesting lecture! Sounds like every business in town will have a booth, including me for my realtor business!"

Alex: "Preen will also have a booth! Get a feather trim or your nails done while browsing!"

Thea: "I am excited! I plan on asking Irene to sign a box of books we can have here at the library."

Mary: "I will be at the first aid booth the whole time. We are offering free bird flu vaccines. I guess I need to buy a new dress for Vincent and Liza's wedding."

Norah: "Same! Irene is so cool! I can't wait to meet her. I also heard that Tara will have a jewelry booth. Oh, and I will, of course, have my food truck ready!"

Goldy: "I heard there will be a swan display?"

Me: "Yes! Charlene said she hired a group called Sassy Swans. They are paid, in Charlene's words, 'to look pretty and swim all day.' They will be at the Hop-In Lake both days."

Mary: "So they are entertainment for the men to look at while the ladies are inside?"

Me: "That is most likely. Haha. Jed's beer truck will be there so they can drink while they ogle the swans."

Thea: "Ok, since we are Irene-focused, let's move on to the book discussion now."

After the book club meeting, I flew to the community center to catch up again on the activities and to get a final lineup of the lectures and a booth guide. I spotted my cousin and center assistant, Vanessa Sparrow, near the front so I flew to her. Then, we both heard loud arguing from inside the center so we both flew in to check it out. We found Charlene and Shelly screaming at each other.

Shelly: "You will pay for stealing Irene from Pheasant Crest!"

Charlene: "I didn't steal anybird! Irene chose to speak here. We aren't paying her a dime to do this. It is all promotional stuff. All proceeds go to the community center! Now go away before I call the police on you for harassment!"

Shelly: "This is public property! You can't do that!"

Charlene: "Watch me!"

Me: "OK, ladies! Enough! Shelly, I think it is best that you fly off now. No need to create even more of a scene."

Shelly: "You birds haven't heard the last of me!"

Shelly flew off in a tizzy.

Charlene: "That bird is insane!"

Vanessa: "She won't leave us alone! Maybe we should hire some security. What do you think Charlene?"

Charlene: "She is all talk and no action. Let's get back

to work. Susan, follow me to my office and I will give you the final booth and lecture list."

I followed Charlene as instructed, then finally made it to the office to file my story for tomorrow. Katherine was in her office, as usual, this time on the phone yelling at some bird. Before I left, I taped a note to her door reminding her to help man the Observer booth at the home and garden show.

Turns out, Charlene should have listened to Vanessa about security. Someone on the lookout would have prevented the disaster that was about to happen.

HOME AND GARDEN SHOW STARTS TODAY

by Susan Towhee
Published March 28, 2023 in the Restful Roost Observer

Today is the day, Restful Roosters! Doors open at 9 a.m. for the first annual home and garden show at the Restful Roost Community Center. The show will be open until 5 p.m. Tickets are $5 for a single-day entry and $8 for a two-day ticket. The full list of booths, lectures, food trucks, and sponsors is below. When you arrive at the show you will be given a map of the center along with specific booth locations.

Booths (location at event hall A):

- Abby's Quality Quilts
- Butterfly Conservation
- Cat Free Restful Roost
- Goldy's Real Estate
- Health Clinic
- Irene Sandpiper
- Millard's Fly Fishing Lures
- Nelson's Nectar
- Norah's Café
- Old Cottontail Mill
- Preen
- Pretty Peacocks Photo Booth
- Rare Orchid info booth (full orchid display in event hall B)
- Restful Roost Honeybee Club
- Restful Roost Inn
- Restful Roost Library
- Restful Roost Observer
- Sassy Swans (swan display at Hop-In Lake)
- Tara's Jewelry
- Vincent's Visions

Lectures (location at event hall C):

March 28

- 10-11 - Caliology Intro and Nest Building 101 with Vincent Vulture
- 1-2 - Cats Be Gone! presented by Cats Free Restful Roost
- 2-3 - Bird-Friendly Coffee with Norah Nuthatch
- 3-4 - *Roosting with Irene* book discussion and signing with Irene Sandpiper

March 29

- 10-11 - Gardening basics with Irene Sandpiper
- 1-2 - Tree ID with Chad Cardinal
- 2-3 - Composting with Vincent Vulture
- 3-4 - Orchid Care with Irene Sandpiper

Food trucks (location at the rear of the community center in front of the Hop-In Lake):

- Norah's Café truck
- Jed's Pub beer truck

Sponsors:
Jed's Pub
Norah's Café
Old Cottontail Mill

Preen
Restful Roost Inn
Restful Roost Observer
Vincent's Visions

Don't forget the nuptials of Vincent Vulture and Liza Vulture from 5-6 p.m. on March 29th at the rare orchid display in event hall B! Everybird is invited!

Happy Spring Restful Roost!

The first day of the show was the most fun Restful Roost has had in a long time! From the booths to the food trucks to the lectures, the day was a hit!

I purchased a new quilt from Abby Mallard, donated to the butterfly conservancy, got my annual bird flu vaccine at the health clinic booth, got my book personally signed by Irene Sandpiper, bought a fly fishing lure from Police Chief Millard Mallard (no, he does not use bird feathers for these!), met traveling salesman Nelson Hummingbird at his nectar booth, took my photo with Adam at the Pretty Peacocks photo booth, tried honey for the first time at the honeybee club booth, bought a beautiful green turquoise bracelet from Tara, and said hello to all my friends who had a booth.

I took shifts and manned both the Observer and the Cat

Free Restful Roost (CFRR) booths. I even spoke a bit at the CFRR lecture on how to get rid of cats from your neighborhood. Leaflets we distributed at human residences seem to be working as more and more cats are being kept indoors. If only the humans knew that birds were behind the outreach!

The Sassy Swans did not disappoint with their splendid beauty. They swam and frolicked in the Hop-In Lake all day. It was a pleasant experience to grab a bite to eat from Norah's Café food truck, enjoy a pint of beer from Jed's beer truck, and watch the swans swim.

Tomorrow was expected to be even more exciting, especially with the wedding as the finale. I was about to find out just how exciting it would be...

The time was 10 p.m. and the police scanner blared to life with an INF call at the Restful Roost Community Center. I had to look that one up as I had no clue what INF was. According to my police book, it had to be an infestation. But, an infestation of what? I flew off to investigate!

I arrived at the community center and heard Charlene yelling. I also heard Vanessa yelling. Then, I heard Vincent yelling. Everybird was yelling! I flew to the noise and found them in event hall B where the orchids were. I looked up and saw bugs flying everywhere! Police Chief Mallard tried to calm everybird down.

Chief Mallard: "Ok, ok! What is going on here? Where the hell did these bugs come from?"

Vincent: "They came from hell, chief!"

Vanessa: "Is this a biblical thing? Should we call a preacher?"

Charlene: "This is disgusting! How do we get rid of them?"

Me: "Hey birds, check this out!"

I saw a box in the corner with a door on it that had swung open. Near it was a small timer. Looks like someone set it to release the bugs.

Chief Mallard: "Well that is where they came from. Not hell. No preacher is needed, but we do need an exterminator."

Charlene: "Oh no! No poison can enter this room! It will damage the orchids! Look, the bugs are already eating through some!"

Vincent: "First, we need to identify the bugs."

A visitor arrived from the side door. It was Irene!

Irene: "Those are aphids, Vincent. We need to get rid of them ASAP!"

Chief Mallard: "Where exactly did you come from, Miss Sandpiper?"

Irene: "I couldn't sleep so I decided to take a walk in your town square. I saw birds flying this way so I flew over, too."

Me: "Did you see anybird flying away from the community center?"

Irene: "No, but I can tell this is sabotage. No aphid was visible when we left for the day."

Vincent: "Well, how do we get rid of them?"

Irene: "Gather up as many birds as you can find. Wake them up! Bring them here and have them eat up as many aphids as they can! Vincent, you and I will trim off all the bad parts that have already been eaten away."

We had a game plan. Chief Mallard, Charlene, Vanessa, and I all flew off to wake up all Restful Roost birds. We flew and chirped that help was needed at the community center. Soon it seemed like every bird species in town was represented at the center to help eat the bugs. We had hummingbirds, chickadees, cardinals, sparrows, vultures, you name it! What bird is going to resist a free all-you-can-eat bug buffet?

After a few hours, all the aphids were gone. Vincent and his assistant, Chad Cardinal, decided to keep watch until morning. Nothing else was going to disturb Vincent's big day! Meanwhile, Chief Mallard pulled me aside and told me he found evidence as to who the culprit was. He had found a Cedar Waxwing feather in the box. Their feathers have a distinctive yellow tip. Only one waxwing was seen recently in the community center. The chief also ~~n~~firmed the security cams had been tampered with.

Shelly was busted! He asked me to not report this until he could confront her and see if he could get a confession. He told me he briefly suspected Irene, but he had a feeling somebird else had a feather in it.

APHID INVASION AT COMMUNITY CENTER

POLICE SEEK SUSPECT IN INFESTATION

RESIDENTS SAVE THE DAY

1ST DAY OF HOME AND GARDEN SHOW A HIT

by Susan Towhee
Published March 29, 2023 in the Restful Roost Observer

Police are asking for tips on last night's aphid invasion at the Restful Roost Community Center. "A bird brought in and released, via a timer, a large amount of aphids in the orchid room," Chief Millard Mallard said. "They would have destroyed the entire orchid display if not for the help of the town to eliminate them and with the help of Miss Irene Sandpiper directing us on what to do."

Restful Roost residents were called to help eat

the nasty bugs. The town responded with great speed. Irene Sandpiper came up with the idea to awaken all birds and have them eat up the aphids before total orchid destruction occurred. "I was happy to help avert a disaster. This has been the best home and garden show I have ever attended. I knew we had to find a way to fix the mess so we can have an even better second day," Irene Sandpiper, guest speaker and author said. "The bird that did this must be caught and jailed!"

Mayor Jed Jaeger had high praise for the town and for Sandpiper. "Last night's horrible infestation was resolved with the help of everybird working together," said Jaeger. "Irene Sandpiper proved why she is the best in the business when it comes to bug identification and eradication as well as plant knowledge and plant care. I plan on naming March 28th Irene Sandpiper Day in Restful Roost."

Please call 555-TWEET if you have any information on this case. Chief Mallard states that he is at a loss for what bird did this and why.

Before the events of the night, the home and garden show recorded record numbers for a day event at the community center. Here are a few highlights of the first day:

- Photo booth where fans could dress up

like a peacock or pose with the Pretty Peacocks

- Very popular Sassy Swan viewings at the Hop-In Lake
- Record sales at Norah's Café food truck and Jed's Pub beer truck
- Informative lectures from local businessbirds Vincent Vulture and Norah Nuthatch
- At capacity lecture on roosting techniques from author and television personality Irene Sandpiper
- Free vaccines provided by the local health clinic
- Informational booths on honeybees, butterflies, and orchids
- Record sales from numerous vendors

Be sure to get your ticket for tomorrow and remember at 6 p.m. to join Vincent Vulture and Liza Vulture as they wed.

Bring your tissues, Restful Roost!

When the doors opened for the second day of the show Police Chief Mallard was right in front ready and waiting to see if Shelly would make an appearance. He hoped the ruse in the article about not having a clue about what happened would bring her over to check out the scene of the crime. Sure enough, Shelly arrived at the ticket line. I walked over to say a quick hello.

Me: "Hi Shelly! So glad you could make it! Hope you can stay the full day so you can see the wedding in the orchid hall tonight!"

Shelly: "You mean the wedding is still on? In the orchid room, you say?"

Guess she didn't read the paper that morning...

Me: "Oh yes, we had a bit of a small disturbance last night, but Irene helped us through that."

Shelly: "Irene! How did she know what to do? I mean, how nice."

Shelly paid for her ticket and walked into the center and straight to the orchid room. Chief Mallard followed a few steps back. Chaos erupted as she saw the beautiful orchid displays. Shelly started screeching and yelling.

Shelly: "This shouldn't look like this! Where is my aphid army? Restful Roost will pay!"

When she started knocking over orchid pots left and right Chief Mallard swooped in and cuffed her wings.

Chief Mallard: “Well, along with your feather I found last night and with that confession, I say we got our bird.”

Shelly: “This isn’t right! This show was supposed to be at Pheasant Crest!”

The crowd watched as Shelly was taken away. Charlene smirked and then instructed the crowd that all was calm and the show must go on!

And what a show it was! The second day was just as event-filled. Vincent gave a composting lecture, Chad provided a great discussion on tree identification, and Irene gave an informative talk on general gardening and orchid care. At the end of the event the wedding began. The swans arrived and flanked the couple as they walked down the aisle. Behind the couple were stunning displays of different colored orchids. Charlene even arranged some to hang from the ceiling. Mayor Jed officiated. Restful Roost Inn owner Peter Woodpecker had a special surprise for Vincent and Liza. He announced a reception in their honor was to be held at the inn immediately after the wedding. All residents were invited.

APHID INVASION CRIMINAL CAUGHT

SHELLY WAXWING IN CUSTODY

RECORD SALES HOME AND GARDEN SHOW

by Susan Towhee
Published March 30, 2023 in the Restful Roost Observer

Restful Roost Police Chief Millard Mallard made an arrest yesterday in the case of the aphid infestation at the home and garden show. Shelly Waxwing, Pheasant Crest community center co-ordinator, was taken into custody after she openly confessed to releasing the aphids. “I also found one of her feathers at the scene of the crime,” Chief Mallard said. “I thank the Restful Roost Observer for holding back on publishing that piece of evidence so I could make a definitive arrest.”

“Criminals will be caught in Restful Roost,” said Mayor Jed Jaeger. “Also, thanks to the great plan to catch the insects, and as mentioned before, I have decided that March 28th will be now known as Irene Sandpiper Day in Restful Roost." Mayor Jaeger said he would present a plaque to Irene at the next home and garden show.

Charlene Chickadee, Restful Roost community center coordinator, was impressed by the show’s success. "I knew it would be special, but the sales and attendance levels blew me away," said Chickadee. "Even with the psycho disturbing the event hall, we got through it and I am currently planning on a 2nd show next year."

Here are a few highlights of day 2:

- All retailers in attendance recorded higher sales than the previous day
- Informative lectures from local business birds Vincent Vulture and Chad Cardinal and author and television personality Irene Sandpiper

"This was a really fun event! We enjoy meeting new people and posing in pictures with them," said Patty Peacock, manager of the Pretty Peacocks. "Sign us up for next year!"

A final highlight of the show was the wedding of Vincent and Liza Vulture. The new couple wed in the orchid event hall at the Restful Roost Community Center. "Vincent knows orchids are my favorite flower. He was so sweet to organize our wedding with the gorgeous orchids in the background," said newlywed Liza Vulture. "I can't wait to spend our anniversaries at the show each year." A reception was held at the Restful Roost Inn following the wedding.

Enjoy the spring Restful Roost!

What made Shelly do it? Was she angry that she couldn't convince Irene to speak at her home and garden show in Pheasant Crest? Did she just have that much animosity for Restful Roost? Was she anti-vulture and wanted to ruin Vincent's big day? Why use aphids? I guess we won't know unless she tells us her reasons. For now, she is locked up in jail. Plans are underway for a 2nd Restful Roost Home and Garden show with Irene Sandpiper as the lead guest speaker.

Just another day in Restful Roost!

~ 3 ~

I THOUGHT I SAW AN IVORY-BILLED WOODPECKER

The Story (as I remember it)...

June 4, 2023

Darkness was approaching at around 9 p.m. and my mate, Adam, and I were deciding on which bourbon to pour while we caught another episode of *Quantum Migration*. When we decided on Colonel Taylor I heard a low voice outside calling my name. It sounded like my boss, Katherine Heron. I peeked outside and saw her sulking by our nest.

Me: "Katherine? Is that you? What are you doing here so late?"

Katherine: "Shh! You have to be quiet. Follow me now

back to the office. There is a major news story that is breaking and I need all wings on deck."

Me: "Ok, let me tell Adam. Can you at least give me a hint?"

Katherine: "No! Say as little as possible."

After a quick goodbye I flew off with Katherine in silence to the Restful Roost Observer office.

Waiting for us at the office was a male Downy Woodpecker. I knew quite a few Woodpeckers, including Peter Woodpecker, who runs the local inn and is a Pileated Woodpecker, but I was not familiar with this bird. Katherine introduced him to me as David. We went to Katherine's office and she locked the door.

Katherine: "David, while I believe your story is complete rubbish, please tell Susan what you told me. If it somehow is true then I need my best reporter on wing to investigate."

David: "I know it sounds crazy, but I know what I saw. My buddy Chad Cardinal was with me and he saw it, too."

Me: "I will keep an open mind Mr. Woodpecker. Just tell me what you and Chad saw. Where is Chad?"

David: "Chad said he was not going to come forward publicly. After he was ridiculed for seeing the UFO last year, he said he wants no more publicity."

Me: "Well he did see a UFO. The whole town did!"

David: "Maybe he will give a statement soon. Chad and I left work together. Vincent Vulture recently hired me to help with the new nest builds. It was a crazy busy day and we were both starving, so we went foraging after work in the Foliage Forest. We both saw something that we could not believe! The bill matched and the wing patterns matched."

Katherine: "Just spit it out!! Tell her what you saw!"

David: "OK! It was an Ivory-billed Woodpecker!"

Me: "Are you serious? Wait, even if you did see one, this isn't even their range! They prefer swampy type environments. Besides, birds and humans have been looking for that bird for decades! What makes you think you saw that bird tonight?"

David: "I know it sounds crazy! We left to get a camera, but when we came back it was gone!"

Katherine: "Because it was never there to begin with! Susan, take their statements, check out the forest, and write up a story. Even if this is hogwash, we need to be on record as having made the first reveal. Use caution. Thank you David for letting us know."

David: "You bet. I hope we see it again!"

David left and Katherine plopped down in her leather chair.

Katherine: "I know he said he and another bird saw it, but that other bird was Chad."

Me: "Well keep in mind Chad saw the same UFO that we did."

Katherine: “Yeah, but Chad also sees his reflection in human vehicle mirrors and tries to fight himself. Nice guy, but not the brightest feather on the wing, if you catch my drift.”

Me: “Alright, alright. We should call Vincent to get his take on David. He will tell us if they are full of malarkey or not.”

Katherine: “Let’s call Mayor Jed as well to let him know.”

Vincent had nothing to say but great things about both Chad and David. He has never witnessed them drinking in excess or discussing tall tales. We woke up the mayor with the news and he thought this could bring worldwide interest to Restful Roost. He asked for a town meeting tomorrow night so the town could devise a plan to work in shifts to spot the woodpecker.

RARE WOODPECKER IN RESTFUL ROOST?

IVORY-BILLED WOODPECKER SIGHTED

RESIDENT CLAIMS HE SAW IT

by Susan Towhee
Published June 5, 2023 in the Restful Roost Observer

Yes, you read that headline correctly, Restful Roosters! A resident came forward last night with a story that even we on staff at the Observer are finding hard to believe!

David Woodpecker told the Observer that he and a friend (who wishes to remain anonymous) spotted an Ivory-billed Woodpecker after work last night. "The bird had the white spots that match the ivory-billed and it had the pale bill," said Finch. "I didn't hear it make a call, though."

David's employer, Vincent Vulture, owner of Vincent's Visions, said David was a valuable employee who could be trusted. "I only hire quality birds who I can rely on," said Vulture. "I stand by David and if he says he saw an ivory-billed, then I believe him."

While we can believe a bird saw something and we can believe that the bird believes, we must take a look at some facts.

The Ivory-billed Woodpecker has not been spotted regularly for many years. Humans have spent untold numbers of hours looking for this bird only to come up with no definite proof that great numbers still exist. Habitat loss means this bird may be extinct, but it has not officially been declared extinct yet. The habitat it did reside in does not match Restful Roost, however. Swamps and heavily wooded areas are its preferred habitats. That makes a sighting here very unlikely, even though one of the last sightings was in nearby Arkansas.

No photo was taken and no sketch was drawn by David or his friend.

Mayor Jed Jaeger has called a town meeting at 7 p.m. tonight at the Restful Roost Community Center. He would like all residents to attend so a plan can be put in place to locate the woodpecker and document it immediately. "If this story is true, then we need proof," said Jaeger.

Do you think the story is real?

Keep your eyes up, Restful Roost!

The phone lines blew up that morning. News organizations, colleges, town residents, you name it, they were calling us asking questions. Even BNN called! The Bird News Network! After an hour, Katherine determined we needed a break, so we flew to the area where David said he saw the bird to take a look ourselves. We saw David and Chad camped out with binoculars, cameras on tripods, and a video camera.

Katherine: "I see you both came prepared this time."

Chad: "I will not be made a fool of again! I refuse to go forward until I have proof."

Me: "Which tree exactly did you see it in?"

David: "That big oak tree right there."

I flew up to get a closer look, but I didn't see any evidence. No recent drill holes, nothing.

Katherine: "Well, keep looking! Maybe the town meeting tonight will help us organize a search of the entire forest. Susan, you can go to your book club meeting which should be starting soon. Then, take the rest of the day off. You were up late last night. I am going back to unplug those damn phones."

I flew over to the library for the book club meeting. This week's book was a cozy mystery by Sheila Connolly. We were re-reading her orchard mystery series. Today's book was the 11th in the series, *A Late Frost*. The usual crowd was in attendance: librarian Thea Bobwhite, Norah Nuthatch, Goldy Goldfinch, Mary Robin, Charlene Chickadee, and Alex Crow.

Mary: "Is it true, Susan?"
Goldy: "Did you see it?"
Norah: "How can you be sure?"
Charlene: "Did it have a mate or was it alone?"
Thea: "Was it as beautiful as I imagined?"
Me: "Ladies! And Alex! I didn't see the bird! Only David Woodpecker and his friend saw it!"
Alex: "Who is the friend? Is he or she a nut job, too?"
Norah: "Alex! Maybe they really did see it!"

Alex: “Honey, a bird that big and loud would have been seen by now!”

Mary: “Proof is needed for sure, but the odds are not good that is really what they saw.”

Me: “I know! I have been reading up on the sightings. It is such a sad story. Humans drove them out of their homes.”

Thea: “We should read a book on them soon! Speaking of books, let’s start on the one we read today. You did read it, Alex?”

Alex: “Yes! I am also reading Sheila’s books on Ireland. I might plan a trip there one day with Peter!”

Charlene: “Speaking of, I stopped by the inn to put up a display for upcoming shows, but the staff said he was out of town.”

Alex: “Yes, he left for a retreat somewhere. Said he needed a break from work. He has been busy lately with all of his managing duties.”

Me: “Well, he might need to head back if word gets out about the ivory-billed. Rooms will be going like hotcakes.”

After more discussion on the woodpecker and what it could look like, Thea brought the group back to the book at hand. After the meeting, I grabbed lunch at Jed’s Pub and went home for a nap. I would need my rest for the town meeting and the search afterward.

The meeting at the community center was wild! Every

seat was taken so many of the birds were standing or perched in the rafters. I would hate to have been sitting under them! Even residents from nearby Thistle Thicket and Pheasant Crest showed up! The mayor gave a quick speech that proof was needed before we could claim that the ivory-billed had returned. He asked for groups of 10 to take a certain section of the forest for an hour at a time. If one person saw something odd they should ask another bird to look. Photos were to be taken if an unknown bird was spotted. Once everyone had their forest tract to monitor, the crowd flew off. Katherine and I joined a group that was to monitor an area by the river. The energy was indescribable! That we might have a bird in town that had not been seen for years was unreal.

A few minutes into our watch, Katherine spotted something!

Katherine: "Look, what is that!"
Me: "I see it! Could it be!?"
Katherine: "Take a photo, quick!"
Me: "Crap, it flew off!"

Soon several other birds flew our way. Among them was the mayor himself.

Jed: "Tell me ya'll saw that! I think that was the ivory-billed!"

Katherine: “Yes, I saw it, too!”

Me: “It flew off before I could snap a photo!”

Jed: “I am going to fly over to the police department to tell Chief Mallard to buy as many video cameras as he can and install them in the forest. We will not miss this bird again!”

Shouting was all around us. Birds were having fun with this! Norah announced she would have her food truck ready in an hour in case birds wanted a cup of coffee or some seeds to nibble on. No bird was going to leave the forest that night! Around 4 a.m. I went back to the office to file my story. I scanned the tree lines as I flew.

MORE RESIDENTS SPOT IVORY-BILLED

RESIDENTS ASKED TO MONITOR FOREST

CAMERAS BEING INSTALLED

PROOF NEEDED

by Susan Towhee
Published June 6, 2023 in the Restful Roost Observer

Restful Roost residents, along with many residents from Thistle Thicket and Pheasant Crest, met last night to organize a non-stop watch in the Foliage Forest for the Ivory-billed Woodpecker. Groups were divided up to take certain parts of the forest and monitor them. "By doing it this way, all parts of the forest will be watched 24-7," said Mayor Jed Jaeger. "We will get a photo if the bird is here." Mayor Jaeger also instructed Police Chief Millard Mallard to install video cameras around the forest to capture any activity.

Observer editor Katherine Heron and I spotted an unusual bird that had distinct markings that matched the ivory-billed, but with no photographic proof, we cannot state for certain what it was.

If anybird has proof of the ivory-billed, please contact the newspaper immediately! Our direct line is 555-NEWS.

Be observant Restful Roost!

By the time my story hit the press, mass hysteria had arrived. When Katherine and I walked out of the Observer office I could see TV networks broadcasting live in the town square. Reporters were everywhere. BNN was set up at the edge of the Foliage Forest. Many birds were being interviewed stating that they saw the bird and were giving descriptions.

Katherine: “This is going to scare the damn bird away!”

Me: “Or we will get proof since we have a ton of cameras here now.”

Katherine: “I know it is 9 a.m., but I need a drink. Let’s go to Jed’s Pub. I have an hour before my next watch session.”

Off we flew.

Working the bar was Jed's assistant, Tara Titmouse. We spotted Peter Woodpecker at the end of the bar so we sat by him to see how his retreat went. Tara walked over to chat and take our orders.

Me: “Hey Peter! Crazy crowd, huh? Must be good for the inn’s business, right?”

Peter: “Hey Susan and Katherine! Yeah, my staff left a voicemail and said we are sold out. Pretty good for a Tuesday! What is all the commotion about outside?”

Tara: “You are kidding, right? Haven’t you heard?”

Peter: “I just flew in an hour ago from my retreat. No TV, phones, or newspapers. I had a complete break from technology. I meditated and was one with nature. It was awesome! Although last night got loud. Seems like the whole town went for a night walk.”

Me: "Um, Peter, where exactly was your retreat?"

Peter: "An isolated section of the Foliage Forest. I was forest bathing."

Katherine: "Oh my god."

Peter: "What? Tell me what is going on!"

Tara: "Here, read the news story in today's paper."

Tara handed him the paper and Peter read and then let out a big piping call.

Peter: "Oh boy. Well, what if it wasn't me they saw? I don't want birds to lose hope!"

Katherine: "It was you. You are a pileated and you look similar to the ivory-billed. It all makes sense now! I am going to ask Thea to stock up on bird ID books at the library!"

Me: "Peter, you need to come forward. We should get this resolved ASAP."

Peter: "Yeah, ok I get it. So much for a restful break. I seem to have caused major drama."

Me: "It isn't your fault. Birds just want to believe. Let's find David and see if he can tell if it was you he saw."

We ate in silence and then flew off to find David's group.

We camouflaged Peter before we left so no one would spot him and cause a scene. Soon we found David and his group near his watch spot. We asked Peter to fly up to the tree and wait.

Me: “Hey David! Any luck?”

David: “Nope, but I am hopeful.”

Katherine: “Hey, do you and the group mind taking a look at that bird up there in that oak?”

We all looked up at Peter who was flashing his wings and calling.

David: “Yep, that looks like a Pileated Woodpecker. Maybe Peter?”

Me: “Yes, that is him. Do you think he is who you saw the other night?”

David: “Susan, I know what different woodpeckers look like. I am one, after all.”

Katherine: “Yes, but he has been in the forest doing a forest shower.”

Me: “Forest bathing.”

Katherine: “Whatever.”

Other members of the group confirmed it was a Pileated. One bird yelled out “Hey Peter! Fly on down here and help us look!”

Peter: “Well, it sounds like they saw something else, ladies!”

David: “Everyone! Be quiet! Look! What is that to the northeast?”

We all looked up and saw a large bird with a white bill and white lines down the back. It soared and then disappeared into the trees. No one thought to take a photo. No one said a word. It was truly a breathtaking moment.

BIRD SIGHTING CONFUSION

PILEATED VS. IVORY-BILLED

SOME CONTINUE TO BELIEVE

ANOTHER IVORY-BILLED SIGHTING?

STORY GENERATES WORLDWIDE FAME

by Susan Towhee
Published June 7, 2023 in the Restful Roost Observer

Restful Roost can rest easy now. Local businessbird, Peter Woodpecker, a Pileated Woodpecker, informed the Observer that he has been in the Foliage Forest the past few days “forest bathing."

“When I go in the forest, I really zone out. I meditate and focus internally,” said Woodpecker.

"I apologize if I confused birds by my appearance. After an hour or so, I fly to a different tree and zone out there. Then, I move on."

Birds that saw the "Ivory-billed" were able to inspect Peter and they have determined that he is possibly what they saw. Some were skeptical, though.

Initial eyewitness David Woodpecker (who first saw the potential ivory-billed) remains adamant that he did see an Ivory-billed Woodpecker. "I know what I saw," said Finch. "And I saw it twice!" Finch and his watch group happened upon another sighting yesterday, but no photo was taken. Also there to witness the potential ivory-billed, was Peter Woodpecker.

The possible sighting of the Ivory-billed Woodpecker brought out reporters from around the globe and renowned college professors from major bird research institutions. While no proof of the bird was found, reporters and professors were able to enjoy the town and brought in extra revenue. "A bit disappointing to find the woodpecker was only a pileated, but, hey, gotta keep the hope alive," said Dr. Gillian Lee from Winger University in Ukraine, who documented the event.

Keep believing Restful Roost!

David Woodpecker to this day remains certain of what he saw. He decided to leave Restful Roost and spend his full time investigating the Louisiana swamps where the ivory-billed Woodpecker was once known to habitat. Chad said he would use his vacation time each year and search with him.

Maybe myself and the others all saw it too that day. It all happened so fast. I can't say for sure that the Ivory-billed is what I saw. As a reporter, I need evidence. As a bird, I need hope. Here's hoping the bird is out there, alive and well.

Just another day in Restful Roost.

A quick note on bird conservation:

As of 2023 hope is still alive for the Ivory-billed Woodpecker. A recent study published in *Ecology and Evolution* proved that the bird may still be out there.

2.9 billion North American birds have vanished since 1970. While the Ivory-billed Woodpecker may be extinct, other birds need our help. Find out how you can help here:

https://www.birds.cornell.edu/home/bring-birds-back/#

~ 4 ~

BIRDS OF A FEATHER DON'T FLOCK TOGETHER

The Story (as I remember it)...

July 16, 2023

The scene was a very crowded Restful Roost library filled with local songbirds, forest animals, and scavenger birds all gathered to hear a Red-Shouldered Hawk give a speech. Yes, you heard that right! A group of birds were in the same room as a hawk! In other words, prey with a predator. However, this was no normal hawk. Town librarian Thea Bobwhite was able to snag world-renowned author Carl Hawk to speak about his new book, *Peace and Harmony Among All Beings.* Thea saw one of his lectures in Los Angeles at a book convention and she convinced him to speak at the Restful Roost library. His book was that week's book club book of the week as well.

Carl's book promoted a friendly lifestyle among all creatures. He writes and speaks all around the world on how hawks should reverse their evolution and move to a herbivore-only diet. He thinks all birds should live in communities together and never ever eat each other. It was quite an interesting and controversial topic. Other hawks did not take too kindly to this ideology and have boycotted his books. Some even show up at Carl's events to protest and burn his books. Thankfully, no unfriendly hawks were here tonight.

Because Carl was a hawk, Mayor Jed Jaeger insisted Police Chief Millard Mallard was in attendance with his many security cameras installed directly at the stage and elsewhere around the venue.

Many in town had most likely not read the book, nor did they intend to buy it, but they couldn't pass up the excitement of seeing Carl and witnessing a hawk up close. The library was at capacity.

After Carl's lively and thought-provoking speech (I mean, could it even be possible in the future?) he asked to shake every bird's wings, pose for pictures, and sign books if anybird wanted that. At first, many birds were skeptical, but my mate, Adam, and I were the first to walk up to greet Carl and thank him for visiting our town. Soon after every bird made their way up to greet Carl.

Local café owner, Norah Nuthatch, supplied snacks and

coffee for distribution after the talk. While everybird was mingling, laughing, and stuffing their beaks all of a sudden the lights went out!

Then, we heard screams! Panic ensued! No bird had any idea what was happening. Did Carl attack? Did he fool us all? Did other hawks start something? I found Thea in the madness and we ran to the basement to find the breaker. We saw it had been turned off so we flipped it back on and ran back upstairs. Now we heard more screams.

"Call the police!"

"Help!"

We approached the stage and found Carl on the floor, gasping for air!

Chief Mallard ran forward.

Chief Mallard: "Alright! Let's have order! We need a doctor! Mary, are you here?!"

Town doctor Mary Robin and her nurse assistant, Simon Sparrow, ran to the stage. Simon began CPR on Carl while an anxious crowd watched. Soon, Carl regained consciousness and said he passed out after drinking a latte. Carl was carried off on a stretcher to the town health clinic for tests. Chief Mallard began the tedious process of interviewing all in attendance and confiscating the food and drink for testing. We were all stunned and hoped for the best for Carl. Norah was embarrassed that her food may have harmed the hawk.

We were soon to find out that something more sinister had occurred.

CONTROVERSIAL HAWK POISONED

BOOK EVENT MARRED BY VIOLENCE

CARL HAWK RECUPERATING

by Susan Towhee
Published July 17, 2023 in the Restful Roost Observer

Carl Hawk, contentious author, and a Red-Shouldered Hawk, was poisoned last night at a speaking event at the Restful Roost library. "After examination, I determined that a puncture mark near the neck was where a poison was injected," said town doctor Mary Robin. "Thankfully, we were able to get Carl to the clinic in time to pump out the poison before it caused a fatality."

Police Chief Millard Mallard will review security cameras and investigate further. "This is clearly an attempted murder," said Chief Mallard. "If anybird saw anything or has any information, they need to come forward now."

While there were many birds in attendance at the packed lecture last night, none witnessed the poisoning. The lights were purposely flipped off while the incident occurred.

Cark Hawk is best known for his latest book, *Peace and Harmony Among All Beings*, which discusses his desire to see all creatures live together with no violence or animosity. Critics of his works claim Carl is preaching against the natural laws of nature and that predators will always need prey. Town librarian Thea Bobwhite, who organized the event was hopeful for a speedy recovery and a quick resolution to who attacked Carl. "Carl has become a friend to me and I sincerely hope no one in the town had anything to do with this. All birds are entitled to their opinions and right to speech," said Thea. "We should have open dialogues about disagreements and not resort to violence."

If anybird has any information please call 55-TWEET.

Be attentive Restful Roost!

To support Norah after she was cleared of having anything to do with the poisoning, many in town, including me, chose to have lunch at her café as a show of support. The chatter was that many hoped it was not a local bird turned crazy. Restful Roost had a great reputation and something like this would spoil it. Word was that Carl was recuperating and had received many flowers and other gifts from locals wishing him well. After lunch, I flew to the police station to get more deets.

I found Chief Mallard hard at work at his desk reviewing security footage.

Me: "Hello chief! Any new leads?"

Chief Mallard: "Hi Susan! Yes, actually. Nothing can be seen in the library because it was too dark due to the lights being out. However, a security camera installed on the top of the city hall building shows a dark figure watching the crowd enter the library from the top of the community center. When I zoom in, I see it is a very large bird. Based on the size of the tail and wings, I would say it is a hawk.

Me: "Wow! So, this is hawk on hawk violence?"

Chief Mallard: "Looks like it, but please hold off on reporting that. I would hate to be wrong. I mean, what if it was Vincent Vulture just taking a look around?"

Me: "Got it. I will keep that under wraps until you give me the green light to publish."

Chief Mallard: "Thanks, Susan. Would you like to fly with me to the clinic? I want to ask Carl some more questions."

Me: "Let's fly!"

We arrived at the clinic to find Mary Robin laughing it up with Carl in his room. A room, I might add, that was filled with flowers, candies, get-well posters, and cards.

Me: "Hello Carl! My name is Susan Towhee. We met at the meet and greet after your talk. Glad to see you are recovering!"

Carl: "Hello! Yes, I remember you. Towhees! What lovely birds! I have also enjoyed your articles in the paper."

Me: "Thank you! Have any idea what bird wanted to do this to you? Have any known enemies?"

Carl: "Ha! You bet I do!"

Chief Mallard: "Any specific threats lately?"

Carl: "Only at every town I go to, except for this one. Restful Roost seems to be quite open to hearing me out."

Mary: "Well we just elected a Pomarine Jaeger as our mayor. Jed moved here from up north a while back. He owns the Pub nearby."

Carl: "How splendid! I must meet him soon!"

Mary: "I am sure that can be arranged, but for now you need more rest. If all looks good I can release you tomorrow."

Chief Mallard: "That is great news, but I am still a bit worried for your safety Mr. Hawk. Can I have a couple of birds stationed at your door tonight just to be safe? Seems like last night there was so much commotion the assailant wouldn't have dared try again. Tonight has me a bit worried, though."

Carl: "Do whatever you like. I am at peace with whatever may happen to me, but I simply could not live if anything were to happen to the staff here at the clinic. They have been so kind to me."

Chief Mallard: "Great. I have two fishing buddies from a couple of towns over who will help out and keep guard here. So, if you see two mean-looking mockingbirds hanging around, that would be them."

Me: "I am going to head back to the office and file my story for tomorrow. Carl, hope to see you out of here soon and we can all get lunch at Jed's Pub!"

I flew off to the office to get some work done, then flew over to the library for research on other stories, and back home for an early dinner with my mate, Adam. I was hopeful Chief Mallard would close this case soon, but with no suspects on his radar yet, I was doubtful.

CARL HAWK TO BE RELEASED TODAY

POLICE CONTINUE SEARCH FOR ATTACKER

TERN MIGRATION LECTURE THIS FALL

by Susan Towhee

Published July 18, 2023 in the Restful Roost Observer

Carl Hawk is set to be released today from the town health clinic. Town doctor Mary Robin said he has made a full recovery. "Carl's strong will to live and hearty body type has helped with his full recovery," said Mary. "I am happy to release him today so he can continue on his lecture circuit."

Police are still searching for the poisoner. When asked for any leads or new information the Observer received a one-sentence statement. "I am still investigating," said Police Chief Millard Mallard.

Please call 55-TWEET with any tips or information.

A tern migration lecture has been announced for August 9 at the Restful Roost Library. Thea Bobwhite, Restful Roost librarian, who will be giving the lecture, announced that the lecture will discuss various migration topics such as typical flight patterns, how to spot food and water, keeping energized, and suggestions on increasing speed. "This lecture will be beneficial for birds that do migrate or for those who want to learn more about those birds that do. Many birds in Restful Roost do not migrate. They are year-long residents of the town. The whole idea of migrating to find food is foreign to them. Learning about what other birds do will be beneficial for all." said Bobwhite. "It will be especially exciting to hear how terns, specifically Arctic Terns, migrate, as some have been known to fly up to 55,000 miles in one year!"

A ticket is not needed for this event, but it is requested that you stop by the library to sign up to attend.

Be observant Restful Roost!

After a couple of hours of work, my editor, Katherine Heron, and I decided to get lunch at Jed's Pub. Carl hadn't been released yet from the clinic so we would have to invite him to lunch on a different day. After a few bites into our worm sandwiches, Jed's police scanner screamed to life with a DIST call at the clinic. Katherine and I looked at each other and flew off. Disturbance at the clinic had to mean Carl was involved.

At the clinic, we saw Chief Mallard along with two mockingbirds waiting outside.

Katherine: "Chief, what happened here?"

Chief Mallard: “Seems like the attacker tried to finish things off today. Luckily my friends here, Frank and Irvin, scared him off.”

Frank: “That SOB blindsided me! Irvin went to get a cup of coffee while I waited at the door. I guess that hawk thought he could handle one mockingbird instead of two. My calls alerted Irvin and he flew over to me and we both dive-bombed that sucker until he flew away!”

Irvin: “Yeah, you can’t get through us! We mobbed him out of town! Not until I was able to get close enough to snag a tail feather!”

Me: “You said hawk. Are you sure it was a hawk that tried to enter the room?”

Chief Mallard: “Oh yeah, Frank, show Susan the feather.”

As soon as I saw it I knew where it came from. A Red-Tailed Hawk!

Katherine: “Wow! So this is hawk-on-hawk savagery!”

Chief Mallard: “Susan and Katherine, I have a plan. Let’s keep this incident under wraps. Don’t mention the feather at all. I think this hawk will try again. Can you post a fake story so we can try to lure the hawk in again? This time, we will be ready to catch him!”

Katherine “You got it, chief. I approve. Susan, go write it up now so we can be ready to publish tomorrow.”

Now we were getting somewhere.

CARL HAWK HELD FOR MURDER SUSPICION

by Susan Towhee
Published July 19, 2023 in the Restful Roost Observer

Carl Hawk has been taken into custody by Police Chief Millard Mallard. "I know he was just released from the clinic after his unfortunate poisoning, but I have evidence that points him to a recent murder in the neighboring town of Thistle Thicket," said Chief Mallard. "I will work with their law enforcement personnel to decide next steps. Carl will be held here at the police station overnight."

No other specifics were provided on the murder, but the Chief is confident they have their bird. More details to follow.

The poisoner is still at large in the poisoning of Carl Hawk at the recent library lecture at the Restful Roost library. Police would still like the public to call if they have information. That number is 55-TWEET.

Stay aware Restful Roost!

Soon after the story made waves around town, a very angry Thea Bobwhite charged into the Observer's office. Katherine and I braced for the onslaught.

Thea: "How dare you print that story today!"

Me: "Just doing our jobs Thea. It was news and it came directly from the police chief."

Thea: "Well, he is wrong! No way Carl would commit murder!"

Katherine: "Maybe Carl duped us all, Thea."

Thea: "I refuse to believe that! This is so upsetting! I need to go back to the library and meditate."

Thea stormed out and slammed the door.

Katherine: "Well, let's just hunker down in here for the day. I want to avoid more scenes like that if we go out and avoid lying to our fellow citizens."

Me: "Sounds like a plan. I will call Jed's Pub and order food. Maybe he or Tara can fly over and drop it off at the front door here."

And that is what we did. Tara tried to pepper me with questions on the phone, but I said I was busy. Katherine and I ate in silence and worked. That silence was disrupted at around 2 p.m. when the police scanner came to life. Another disturbance call and this time at the police station. Off we flew!

A crowd had gathered at the police station as we arrived. We immediately saw the mockingbirds and Chief Mallard gathering up a large net near the back of the station. Caught up inside was a large Red-Tailed Hawk! They got him!

Me: "Tell me what happened chief!"

Chief Mallard: "Well, I installed this great contraption last night by the back door. It was set to trap whatever stepped in it. No one here uses the back door, so I figured the hawk would try there first to be sneaky. I loudly asked Frank and Irvin if they wanted lunch at Jed's. I said the prisoner would be ok alone for the time being. We flew in that direction and then hunkered down on Jed's roof with binoculars to wait and see."

Irvin: "Yea, and this dumbass fell for it!"

Frank: "Yeah, he flew right in and panicked and got his feathers all ruffled. Say, what is your name buddy?"

The hawk eyed them all menacingly.

The Hawk: "I want a lawyer."

POISONER OF CARL HAWK CAPTURED

RED-TAILED HAWK IN CUSTODY

CARL HAWK OPTS NOT TO PRESS CHARGES

by Susan Towhee
Published July 20, 2023 in the Restful Roost Observer

A Red-Tailed Hawk was caught yesterday trying to break into the Restful Roost police station. "With the help of the Observer and two local hired bodyguards, we were able to catch the attacker of Carl Hawk," said Chief Mallard. "I designed a ruse to make the criminal think Carl was being held at the police station. When he tried to attack Carl again we were prepared and caught him in a trap net. A feather was taken from the hawk while in pursuit by two mockingbirds on the previous day and there is a feather missing from the one arrested." Chief Mallard confirmed the Red-Tailed Hawk was the poisoner of Carl Hawk due to the pack of syringes he found with the hawk.

The Observer's article yesterday was part of the chief's plan to deflect the actual whereabouts of Carl Hawk. Carl was held safely in a suite at the Restful Roost Inn until the plan concluded. The chief would like to thank Peter Woodpecker,

Restful Roost Inn owner, and two local mockingbirds who greatly assisted in the ploy, Frank and Irvin Mockingbird.

The Red-Tailed Hawk has not made any statements but has asked for legal representation. Carl Hawk has chosen not to press charges, so Chief Mallard stated the hawk will be dropped off at a local human raptor rehab center. "The hawk does have some wing damage from flopping around in the trap. Best to just drop him off somewhere so he can get the care he needs," said Chief Mallard.

Carl Hawk is thankful for the quick resolution on the attack and hopes to visit Restful Roost again soon. "I am quite impressed with the attention given to my assault. It means a lot that songbirds, ducks, woodpeckers, you name it, all came together to help me," said Carl. "I know the dangers I face saying the things I say. I will take steps in the future to ensure my safety and the safety of my fans."

Love each other Restful Roost!

Another season went by and another crime was resolved.

The Red-Tailed Hawk healed and refused to leave the

raptor center. The humans have adopted him as their pet and have even featured him as their new logo on brochures that they pass out. Maybe he read a bit of Carl's book on peace among species and took it to heart.

Carl hired Frank and Irvin Mockingbird as his bodyguards for the rest of his book tour. They were excited to fly and see the world. For his second book, Carl announced that he and Thea will team up to write a book on the events in Restful Roost as a real-life example of interspecies cooperation. I am sure it will be on our book club list one day.

Just another day in Restful Roost!

~ 5 ~

DUMP AND CHASE

The Story (as I remember it)...

October 1, 2023

Well, it was the first of October and no abductions, rare bird sightings, poisonings, etc. were reported in August or September. It was a rather calm end of the summer. Restful Roost summers bring in the tourists who visit our Foliage Forest, water ski on the River, take in a show at our community center, or book a spa day at the Restful Roost Inn. Police Chief Millard Mallard's hundreds of video cameras installed around town have done their job of keeping the place crime-free. Birds felt calm and at peace in town.

So, I was surprised when I received a call from my boss, Katherine Heron, at around 9 p.m. to report immediately to the newspaper's office for breaking news straight from the mayor. What could possibly have happened now, I thought?

I arrived to find Katherine, Mayor Jed Jaeger, Restful Roost Community Center Events Coordinator Charlene Chickadee, local businessbird and architect Vincent Vulture, and a large Canada Goose seated in our conference room.

Katherine: “Susan! Thanks for heading over at short notice.”

Me: “No problem! Tell me what crazy crime has happened now.”

Jed: “Oh, nothing nefarious going on, Susan! I have a major announcement.”

Me: “Oh, no. Please don’t tell us you are planning on running for governor or something.”

Jed: “Hell no. I am happy here in Restful Roost. I have no plans for higher office! I am excited to announce that over the summer I bought Restful Roost a hockey team!”

Me: “Wow! That is so cool!”

Charlene: “Yep! Vincent and I were in on the secret. Over the last couple of months, we have been planning how to add an ice rink to the community center, build dressing rooms, install spectator seating, etc.

Vincent: “It has been quite a fun project! Something I have never done before!"

Jed: “Everybird, please meet the coach of the new hockey team, Gary Goose!”

Gary: “It is so nice to meet all of you! I can’t wait for

my boys and girls to hit the ice! So, a little background, we were all playing in Mooselick, Canada. Funding fell through for our salaries and upkeep on the rink due to the local mayor there swindling public funds. Ya see, he had a mistress and he was using taxpayer money to buy her fancy cars, expensive jewelry... well, you get the picture. We had to find another place to play before the new season started. Mayor Jed here reached out and offered us a deal and here we are! Plus, the warmer weather would be a welcome change!"

Katherine: "So when will the first game be? And what will you all be called?"

Jed: "We are aiming for October 15 as the first game. That gives us enough time to sell tickets and get the rink ready. I came up with the name. They will be called the Restful Roost Rocs!"

Vincent: "Ah, named for the mythological bird! Love it!"

Jed: "Yep! I even crafted a beer at the pub in honor of the team. The Roc Bock!"

Me: "I can't wait to try it! This is going to be fun having our own team to cheer for!"

Katherine: "Susan, write up the story for print tomorrow."

Jed: "Let's have a meet and greet outside the community center tomorrow so the town can meet the coach and the team. I will have my beer truck set up. See if Norah can provide those lame seeds and grass she sells for the other birds."

I stayed for a bit to complete my story. Who knew in

the days to follow that the simple idea of having a hockey team in town would create controversy, confusion, and a horrid stench?

HOCKEY COMES TO RESTFUL ROOST

MAYOR JAEGER BUYS TEAM

NAME TO BE RESTFUL ROOST ROCS

OCTOBER 15 FIRST GAME

MEET AND GREET TONIGHT

by Susan Towhee
Published October 2, 2023 in the Restful Roost Observer

Ice hockey has arrived in Restful Roost! In a surprise announcement, Mayor Jed Jaeger informed the Observer that over the summer a purchase of a hockey team was made. "We had a huge surplus in our budget and with those funds, I made a bid on a bankrupt team from Mooselick, Canada," said Jaeger. "The team had an excellent record, but due to horrible mayoral practices there, the city could no longer afford them. Having this team here will allow even more tourist dollars to flow in. Birds can visit in the fall and winter and have something to do now at our community center during the colder months."

The deal was a closely kept secret between the mayor, the coach (Gary Goose), Restful Roost Community Center Events Coordinator Charlene Chickadee, and local businessbird and architect Vincent Vulture.

Vulture is confident the center will be ready for the first game. "This is a first for me as far as planning a hockey rink, but I have done my research," said Vulture. "This week we will have the cooling units in, the dressing rooms complete, and the rink outlined and filled with water and frozen by next week."

Charlene Chickadee is excited to add more events to the center's schedule. "The colder months are always a bit sparse when it comes to events," said Chickadee. "This will bring excitement to the town and draw in our more sports-minded birds."

Coach Goose was fired up when asked for a comment. "I am so excited to be a Restful Rooster now! The weather here is fantastic and I know my boys and girls will love playing here! Come out and see us whoop the Henrietta Howling Hens on the 15th," said Goose.

Here is a bit of information on our new team:

- Named the Restful Roost Rocs (name courtesy of our mayor) after the large mythic bird in human folklore
- The roster is all Canada Geese, including their coach
- The team was last stationed in Mooselick, Saskatchewan, Canada
- The Rocs will be part of the SPBHL - Southern Professional Bird Hockey League

There will be a meet and greet tonight at 7 p.m. outside the Restful Roost Community Center. Stop by and meet the Rocs! Norah's Café will be on hand serving food and Jed's Pub will have a beer truck serving their brand new beer made just for the team, the Roc Bock! Also, be sure to stop by the community center box office to get your tickets!

Let's drop the puck, Restful Roost!

After a few hours of work, Katherine let me off early so I flew to my nest to get my mate, Adam, and we had an early dinner at Jed's Pub. We had to try that new Roc Bock beer! We stayed until 7 p.m. so we could attend the meet and greet which was a ton of fun! We met all the new players and chatted with them about Canadian life. A few even met the human leader, Prime Minister Trudeau, when they visited Ontario. We took photos, signed up for season tickets, had a few more beers, and then headed home.

The days went by and construction continued on the rink, dressing rooms, and seats. Vincent and his crew were hard at work so all could be complete by the 15th. Everybird was anticipating the opening day.

ROCS OPENING NIGHT TONIGHT

SOLD OUT GAME

by Susan Towhee
Published October 15, 2023 in the Restful Roost Observer

Does everybird have their tickets for opening night? If not, you are out of luck because tonight's game is sold out!

For those attending, doors open at 6 p.m. Concession stands will be ready and open on the concourse. Get your Rocs jersey at the Pro Shop by section 1. Questions or issues during the game? Stop by the Fan Info Center at section 2.

The puck drops at 7 p.m. as the Restful Roost Rocs take on the Henrietta Howling Hens.

Let's go Rocs!

Game time! It was a packed house at the community center for the first game. Having our own team to cheer on certainly brought out the town. It had also brought out quite a powerful stink. I wondered if having that many birds in one place was the cause of the smell, but I then remembered many a packed night at the center for sold-out shows. No, this stink was something else. Everybird was talking about it. Maybe Vincent hit a sewer line when doing construction. I made a plan to visit the info center at the end of the first period to see if Charlene or her assistant, Vanessa, knew what the stench was.

When I arrived at the info center many other fans were there complaining about the smell. Vanessa was manning the desk and trying to calm the birds down.

Vanessa: "I am aware of the smell. Charlene is trying to figure it out. We hope to have it resolved by the beginning of the first period. Now, everyone grab a coupon to get 50% off a beer at the concession stand, and be sure to get back to your seat quickly so you can see the Rocs add to their 3-0 lead!"

Angry bird 1: "This is ridiculous. With the stank in the air, I won't be able to taste the beer!"

Angry bird 2: "Yea! Can I get free nachos instead?"

Angry bird 3: "I demand to know what is happening! Now!"

I left Vanessa and the info center after grabbing my beer coupon. No need to question Vanessa more and add to her stress tonight. She and Charlene were aware and working on it. Why did birds have to be so rude?

By the end of the 2nd period, the smell seemed to have worsened. My mate, Adam, and I tried to determine what it could be. A mixture of poop, stagnant water, and wet grass is what it smelled like. I went back to the info center to see if the source was identified.

Angry bird 1: "I want my money back! I can't enjoy the game!"

Charlene: "The Rocs are up 5-0! How can you not enjoy that? I know the place smells! Please be patient while we figure this out. Here, take a face mask. The health clinic dropped them off for birds to use."

Angry bird 2: "I don't want to wear that! I want my money back!"

Vanessa: "Here, sign your name on this paper and we will be in touch regarding refunds."

A very loud and pissed-off Mayor Jed Jaeger stormed in. Along with him was Vincent Vulture.

Jed: "We will not give refunds. You already saw half of the game. Bird up and finish the game. These ladies are trying to help. Stop yelling and go back to your seats."

That seemed to help as the angry birds all walked away quietly. I stayed back to get the scoop. When we had the room to ourselves the mayor started his questioning.

Jed: "What in the world is going on here? Vincent, did you break the toilets?"

Vincent: "I didn't touch any sewage lines or mess with the toilets!"

Charlene: "The smell seems worse by the locker rooms. Can you go check there to see if you can find anything out?"

Vincent: "Sure thing. On it now!"

Jed: "Charlene, go on the speaker system and tell birds we will get this resolved before the next game. Tell them the fan information center is closed and we will see them all at the next game."

Charlene: "Oh thank you, Jed! That makes our night easier."

Me: "What do you want me to put in the paper to-morrow about this?"

Jed: "Just say we are working on it. If we don't know, we don't know!"

I made it back to my seat just as the puck dropped for the 3rd period. I had my mask on and brought one for Adam. It didn't help at all with the smell in the air, but the smell of victory was pretty sweet. Rocs 7 and Hens with a big egg.

7-0 BLOWOUT

ROCS SCORE FIRST WIN WITH SHUTOUT

MYSTERIOUS SMELL AT GAME

by Susan Towhee
Published October 16, 2023 in the Restful Roost Observer

The Restful Roost Rocs wrapped up their first game last night at the Restful Roost Commu-nity Center with a 7-0 win against the Henrietta Howling Hens. Team captain Derek Goose scored

2 goals with 5 other Rocs completing the scoring. "What better way to start the season than with a strong win," said Coach Gary Goose. "We will keep the momentum going for our next game in one week!"

Fans cheered on the team all night and bought up brand-new Rocs jerseys in the pro shop. "I love that hockey has arrived in Restful Roost! It will make the boring winters fun" said Restful Roost resident Chad Cardinal.

While fans enjoyed the on-ice action, off the ice and in the air was a different story. Many fans complained about a mysterious smell that permeated the air in the center. Charlene Chickadee, Restful Roost Community Center Events Coordinator, said she is working on finding the root of the issue and fixing it. "We are working with our rink designer, Vincent Vulture, to help find the cause and remedy the stink before the next game," said Chickadee. "We appreciate the patience of our fans."

Go Rocs!

Later that morning, I made my way to the library for the weekly book club meeting after filing my story at the office. The book that week was *All the Way: My Life on Ice* by Jordin Tootoo. Tootoo was a human ice hockey player and a big inspiration to many of the players on the Rocs, so our librarian made sure we had copies to enjoy. After the lively discussion about the smell at the game, I decided to fly back to the office. Before I was about to take flight, Charlene asked if she could have a word with me.

Charlene: Susan! We found the source of the stink!

Me: "That's great! Will it be easy to get rid of?"

Charlene: "Well, yes, but I don't know how to handle the...situation."

Me: "What do you mean?"

Charlene: "Well... Vincent and I found piles of...um... geese scat in the dressing room and cafeteria the players use."

Me: "Oh my! Well, that explains it. Piles, you say?"

Charlene: "Yes! I have never seen so much crap!"

Me: "Just tell them to poo elsewhere. It will cause a bacteria outbreak if you don't."

Charlene: "I don't want to embarrass them or drive them away."

Me: "If it will hurt ticket sales then you won't be the one driving them away. It will be the fans!"

Charlene: "Ugh, you are right."

Me: "Look, let's go talk to the mayor. Let's also stop by the health clinic and get Mary. I know she just left the book club, but we can catch her. She can help explain the health risks as well. Then, we can all discuss it with the coach. He can be the one to tell the players to stop."

We flew to get Mary and then met with the Mayor in

his office at city hall. All agreed this was an issue. Mary said she would compile an info sheet for the coach so he could review it and give it to the players. If not controlled, the scat could cause health issues among the rest of the birds in town. An afternoon meeting at the community center was planned to go over the news.

Around 4 p.m. we all met with the Coach in a conference room. The stench was overpowering. Vincent Vulture joined us as well.

Charlene: "Thanks all for attending this meeting. Coach, we have some difficult news to share with you, but we hope you will be open to what we have to say."

Gary: "Oh, no! You all are kicking us out already! I knew it was too good to be true!"

Jed: "Hold up! No one is kicking you out. However, if we don't do something about this stinky ice rink, no one will come back to games!"

Gary: "What do you mean stinky?"

Vincent: "Oh come on! I am a vulture, and even I think it smells revolting in here!"

Mary: "Please, understand. Gary might be used to the smell and he is probably a bit confused as to what we are talking about."

Charlene: "Gary, Vincent and I found large piles of, um, you know.."

Jed: "Shit, Gary! You and your players have been shitting where you eat! It's gross, dude."

Gary: "What do you mean? We all poop. That's what we do. We eat and poop."

Vincent: "Well you could do it elsewhere."

Gary: "We can't control when we poop. It just comes out!"

Vincent: "If it just comes out, then why aren't you pooping on the ice? We only found it in the dressing room and cafeteria you all use."

Gary: "Only blood is spilled on the ice!"

Vincent: "Whatever!"

Gary: "You mean all the other birds here poo in a special area? Give me a break! I have seen birds squirt it out when they like and where they like."

Mary: "Songbird, sparrow, and other smaller birds' scat are quite smaller than Canada Geese scat. I think what we need to focus on here is the amount of the poo you and the players produce each day. Gary, Restful Roost has not had any Canada Geese visits, so we are just not aware of your eating and digestion habits. A typical goose can poop up to several times in an hour and up to 20 times a day."

Charlene: "Oh my god. Multiply that by 20 players and a coach."

Mary: "Yes, it can pile up, unfortunately. Many other birds have runnier, liquidy-type excretions. Because of the grassy diet of geese, their scat can be larger and more solid. Another issue, Gary, is that large amounts of fecal matter can cause illnesses due to the bacteria."

Gary: “Oh, so now you are saying we are making birds sick!”

Jed: “No one is saying that. We just want to make sure that doesn’t happen. We also need the smell to be controlled so birds can enjoy the game without wearing a gas mask! What can we do here, Mary? Change their diets?”

Mary: “Of course not! The geese just need to be trained to poop in a central area so it can be maintained. We already know it can be done because Gary said they know not to poop on the ice.”

Charlene: “You mean like a human bathroom?”

Jed: “That is degrading!"

Vincent: “Hey, I have an idea! What about a compost pile? We could use the poo, along with seed cases from Norah’s Café and leaves from the Foliage Forest, to fertilize a flower garden we could plant in the back of the community center.”

Charlene: “What a great idea! Coach, your player’s poo can help beautify the center grounds!”

Jed: “I love this! It can be marketed as the player’s helping out the community!”

Mary: “Who will be in charge of scooping the scat? Whatever bird does it needs to be very careful and sanitary.”

Jed: “How about Charlene and her helper, Vanessa?”

Charlene: “Um, no! I am not scooping poo. Neither is Vanessa. That is not in our job descriptions!”

Me: “Coach, can the players scoop it? It is their fecal remains.”

Gary: “Well, I guess that would be the best option. And,

I guess since we are in your town and using your facility, we gotta play by your rules."

Jed: "Great! Susan, the only thing I ask is that we kind of keep this on the down low. It may cause ridicule for the players and embarrass them that they have to scoop their own poo. We don't make other birds do this."

Me: "Sorry, mayor! I gotta print the facts!"

With that the meeting ended. A plan was put in place and all parties were happy. The community center crew got a cleaner facility, Vincent got a garden, Gary was able to stay in town, and the mayor got to keep his hockey team. I flew to the office to file my story."

MYSTERIOUS SMELL ID'D

GEESE SCAT THE CULPRIT

SCAT TO BE USED FOR GARDEN

by Susan Towhee
Published October 17, 2023 in the Restful Roost Observer

The overpowering smell at the recent Rocs hockey game at the Restful Roost Community Center has been identified. Charlene Chickadee, center events coordinator, informed the Observer that piles of geese scat were found in the dressing rooms and in the cafeteria the players use. The piles were located close to air vents so that is why the smell wafted through the rink. "The piles of scat caused the strong smell. Scat of this magnitude is just not something we are used to here in Restful Roost," said Chickadee.

Town doctor Mary Robin said the piles of scat could be harmful if not removed and cleaned up. "Geese can eliminate multiple times a day and their scat can contain and spread bacteria that can be harmful to birds and even humans," said Robin. "A proper disposal method is recommended to avoid a disease outbreak."

A happy ending to this story is that the Rocs players will be responsible for cleaning up their scat and contributing it to a compost pile behind the center. The compost will be used to fertilize a new flower garden to be located next to the Hop-In Lake behind the community center. The idea to turn refuse into reward came from local businessbird, Vincent Vulture. "I thought, hey, we have all of this great manure, so what better way to use that than for a garden," said Vulture.

Coach Gary Goose was proud of his team stepping up to help the community. "The players are happy to help pretty up the town with a new garden. They know, as well as I do, that the garden will essentially be theirs. Our creations will help make beautiful flowers grow. How cool is that?" said Goose.

The second Rocs game is tonight. The existing scat has been removed and the rink has been sanitized. No new smells have been reported by center staff. If you haven't purchased a ticket, stop by the box office before they are all gone! Come out and support your Restful Roost Rocs!

GO ROCS!

It had been a few weeks since I filed that story. The Rocs were still on a win streak and the rink only smells of fresh ice and popcorn from the concession stands. Vincent says the compost pile is on track to create a large garden for the spring and he may even have enough left over to ship to other towns.

Just another day in Restful Roost!

~ 6 ~

IRRUPTION DISRUPTION

The Story (as I remember it)...

December 22nd, 2023

The time was about 8 p.m. and my mate, Adam, and I had just poured another glass of bourbon while we sat by the fire pit near our roost. We had human singer Chris Isaak's album *Christmas* playing. A light snow had started to fall. It was definitely enough to put you in a holiday spirit. All of a sudden we heard a loud rustling sound above us. Was it another UFO? A wind storm? Santa? We looked up to see a very large flock of birds. They were approaching the center of town and looked to make a landing! Adam and I took flight and followed them. A mass migration in December? Something was up!

When we arrived at the town square it was completely filled with birds! As I approached them to get a closer look I saw they were all Evening Grosbeaks. The males don pretty black and yellow colors with white patches in the wings and the females are a bit more drab, but still very beautiful.

By this time, the commotion had attracted a large crowd, including the mayor, Jed Jaeger.

Jed: "What is the meaning of this? What are all of these birds doing here? Who is the ringleader?"

The "ringleader" approached the mayor and offered his wing as a form of a greeting.

Male Grosbeak: "Hello Mayor Jaeger! My name is Elvis Grosbeak. Sorry to disturb you and your pleasant town, but we are here in search of food. You see, we came from up north and this winter has been a doozy! With climate change, we just can't depend on reliable food sources year to year. I gathered my buddies and we decided to fly south. You see, I love Elvis Presley! Even changed my name to match his! We are making our way to see his home Graceland."

Jed: "Well, ya'll need maps. This ain't Memphis."

Elvis: "Right, we are aware of that, but we needed to stop a bit for a rest. We read about one of our favorite hockey teams moving here and thought we could catch a game and get our strength back for a few days before we travel to Memphis. We also heard the rumors about a Pomarine Jaeger being the mayor and we had to see it for ourselves. You, Mr. Mayor, are a legend up north!"

Jed: "Flattery will get you nowhere! What do you mean you will stay a few days? You will diminish all of our food supplies! There have to be hundreds of you! Humans who provide seed during winter will get fed up and stop putting food out"

Thea Bobwhite, our town librarian, spoke up.

Thea: "Actually, Mayor Jed, humans may enjoy this. See, I have read that humans like it when large groups of birds appear that usually aren't from around here. They call it an "irruption" and they get real excited about it."

Jed: "A what? Eruption? Isn't that a Van Halen song?"

Me: "No! Irruption! It starts with an I! Look, Jed, it is the holiday season. Have a heart. These birds are tired and they need food."

Elvis: "We promise we won't be a burden!"

Jed: "Ok, I guess so. I mean think of the revenue this can bring to Restful Roost. I do think we need to alert the town to your presence and why you are here. You did wake up almost the whole town. Maybe we can do a meet and greet at the community center tomorrow? We can answer any questions the residents have.

With that, the crowd dispersed to finish their night's sleep. It was very exciting to have a new flock of birds in town. I couldn't wait to learn more about them and hear about their travels! Adam and I flew home to finish our drinks and discuss what we just saw. We were both thankful that we had humans near us to provide additional food when we needed it. Some birds just aren't so lucky.

IRRUPTION!

FLOCK OF GROSBEAKS ARRIVE IN TOWN

SHARING OF FOOD ENCOURAGED

MEET & GREET TONIGHT

by Susan Towhee
Published December 23, 2023 in the Restful Roost Observer

Restful Roost has new visitors! Around 500 Evening Grosbeaks arrived in our town last night. The grosbeaks are in search of food due to minimal resources in their homeland up north. Their stay is only temporary as they are headed to Memphis next week. Leader of the pack, Elvis Grosbeak, said they planned the stop in Restful Roost en route to Memphis because they loved the hockey team that recently moved here from Canada. "We hope we can catch a game while we are here," said Grosbeak. "We have heard such great things about this town. I know we will enjoy our stay."

Town librarian Thea Bobwhite provided information as to why these "irruptions" occur. "When an environment runs low on food supply, some birds will decide to leave their winter roosting grounds and fly to warmer regions where a more abundant food supply may be found," said Bobwhite. "These are called irruptions. It is all about survival. These grosbeaks need food and we should help them out. One day it might be us in search of food in Mexico."

Restful Roost residents are encouraged to help share the feeders with the grosbeaks and offer food from their caches to any visitor they meet.

Have a question about grosbeaks? Want to meet one? Stop by the Restful Roost Community Center tonight at 7 p.m. to meet the grosbeaks. Norah's Café will be serving brand new suet cakes and Abby Mallard will offer holiday-themed seed wreaths.

Be generous, Restful Roost!

That morning I flew to the library for our weekly book club meeting. Thea had us reading *The Garden Plot*, book one in the Potting Shed mystery series. I enjoyed the

British gardening setting in that one. The usual crew was in attendance along with Thea and myself: Norah Nuthatch, Goldy Goldfinch, Mary Robin, Charlene Chickadee, and Alex Crow. Charlene provided some insight into our new grosbeak friends.

Charlene: "All of the grosbeaks are excited for the meet and greet tonight. Some were a little scared to meet the mayor, but I told all of them Jed was harmless. They really love hockey! Elvis especially! He knew all the players' stats and bios. They are all excited about attending the next game."

Alex: "Where are all of these new birds going to sit for the game? Isn't the season sold out?"

Charlene: "That is something we are working on. I was going to see if any season ticket holders want to get a refund for one game so we can help fit the grosbeaks in."

Thea: "No way! We want to enjoy the game with them!"

Me: "It will be pretty cold this week. Could we move the game outside? Maybe have an outside game?"

Goldy: "Great idea! How about we freeze the Hop-In Lake and have the game there?"

Charlene: "That is not a bad idea!"

Norah: "I can sell hot chocolate!"

Mary: "Luckily we have a world-class architect in town who can set that up! I am sure Vincent will accept that challenge."

Charlene: "It will be a challenge for me, too! Ladies, and Alex, I gotta fly off and present this to Vincent. We will have a lot of work to do if we decide to pull this off! See ya'll at the meet and greet tonight!"

We finished up the book discussion and went our separate ways. I flew off to the office to fill my boss, Katherine Heron, in on the outdoor game idea. This would be a first for the town!

While at the office, I filled Katherine in on the book club gossip and we caught up on cleaning and getting things organized so we could start 2024 with a clean slate. After today the office would be closed for the holiday season until the first of the year. She also proposed an assignment for me that I couldn't refuse.

Katherine: "Susan! There is an idea for a news story that has been brewing in my head for a while. I always dreamed of writing it up, but I am getting up there in years and I need young blood to take this one. Now, it will require a lot of time and a lot of travel. The story is important, though and it needs to be told. Plus, you just might get a Pulitzer out of this."

Me: "OK, I am open to hearing what this is."

Katherine: "It may be a bit dangerous. Still in?"

Me: "I wouldn't call myself a journalist if I wasn't willing to get my wings dirty."

Katherine: "Great! I want you to fly around the world and report on the strange bird dishes that humans eat. I know humans eat chickens, turkeys, etc., but this is about the really weird stuff. Like bird's nest soup, foie gras, and the horrible ways they eat those poor buntings in France."

Me: "Oh, wow. That sounds very interesting. And a bit depressing. Why the interest in reporting on these dishes? It won't change humans' minds on what I report."

Katherine: "No, but we need to educate birds on what is happening. Maybe if enough of us know about it, we can make a difference. If birds know about how humans steal their nests for soup, maybe we can convince enough swiftlets to make their nests somewhere where humans can't get them. Or, if more geese know they are only being force-fed so they will be killed just for their livers, maybe they will start a hunger strike where they are held and humans will stop with that evil practice."

Me: "I like your thinking. We can also try to educate humans. It worked with our Cat Free Restful Roost project! Leaflets and flyers can be dropped in areas where these atrocities are happening. Then, maybe humans will see how their actions are affecting birds. So when do you want me to start this project?"

Katherine: "We can talk more about it when we get back from the holiday break, but I want you to be gone the entire summer. Then, you can write up a report during the fall. Sound good?"

Me: "Yes, it does. I accept your offer."

Katherine: "Perfect! Now, let's fly to get some lunch and a beer at Jed's!"

With that, we flew out of the office en route to Jed's.

However, we didn't make it as quick as we wanted to. We were distracted by a commotion near the Foliage Forest. A group of humans were gathered with binoculars and a film crew was set up. They had found the grosbeaks!

Me: "How about that! Thea was right! Humans love the irruption!"

Katherine: "It's like the spotting of the Ivory-billed Woodpecker again. People are everywhere! Look, that guy has a Cornell Lab of Ornithology hat on. This is a big deal!"

Me: "So cool! Haha, check it out, Elvis is fanning his tail at the humans!"

Katherine: "That guy is a hoot! Let's grab that beer and food now."

Katherine and I enjoyed our lunch and then she let me have the rest of the day off. I had to tell Adam about the summer plans Katherine had for me. She was after a Pulitzer for the paper. We came real close last year to winning one for a story we did on a corrupt Blue Jay that ran for mayor here. Word was we narrowly lost the prize to a paper in New Mexico. The *Hatch Dispatch* won for a story on roadrunner trafficking near the border. Soon, Adam and I left for the meet and greet. Luckily it would be dark by then, so the humans would be gone. If not, they would have surely followed the grosbeaks to our community center. The center was a place for birds and birds only!

At 7 p.m. the Restful Roost Community Center was packed and loud! Mayor Jaeger welcomed the grosbeaks to town. Charlene introduced Elvis to the crowd and he spoke about his life up north for a bit. He said he loved the southern food and Elvis Presley. He got the crowd singing a very vibrant rendition of *Viva Las Vegas*. That grosbeak can sing!

Norah's food truck was a hit. She sold a special berry suet cake mix she made up just for the grosbeaks. Abby Mallard, now the wife of Police Chief Millard Mallard, made some beautiful Xmas wreaths made out of various seeds. The proceeds of sales from the suet cakes and wreaths would go to a fund to help pay the admission price for all grosbeaks to the Graceland grounds. Norah knew a family of woodpeckers who lived at Graceland that give tours and they offered a deep group discount. All grosbeaks squeaked in approval when that announcement was made! This prompted Elvis to grab the mike and lead another sing-along, this time the crowd sang a rocking version of *All Shook Up* in honor of Norah and Abby.

Once the crowd quieted down Charlene took the stage again and said she had a major announcement. She proceeded to tell the crowd that tomorrow night's game would be an outdoor game at the Hop-In Lake so all residents and grosbeaks could attend. Cheers exploded through the center! An Xmas Eve outdoor hockey game! Only in Restful Roost!

OUTDOOR HOCKEY GAME TONIGHT

GROSBEAKS WELCOMED BY TOWN

by Susan Towhee
Published December 24, 2023 in the Restful Roost Observer

Restful Roost knows how to throw the welcome mat down for guests! Last night a festive gathering occurred at the Restful Roost Community Center. The visiting grosbeaks mingled with residents to answer questions about northern climates and migration patterns. Food was offered in the form of suet cakes by Norah's Café and seed wreaths by Abby Mallard. The proceeds of sales from Norah's cakes and Abby's wreaths will help pay for ticket costs to visit the home of human singer Elvis Presley. The grosbeaks will be traveling to Memphis just for a visit to a place called Graceland, where Elvis lived. Grosbeak group leader, Elvis Grosbeak (no relation to the singer) said he was moved and humbled by the generosity and kindness of Restful Roosters. "No place we have visited has welcomed us like Restful Roost has," said Grosbeak. Elvis led the crowd in fun and lively sing-alongs of human Elvis's songs during the event.

Charlene Chickadee, Restful Roost Community Center Coordinator, announced the Hop-In Lake behind the center will be frozen to accommodate an outdoor hockey game to be played tonight. Local businessbird and town architect Vincent Vulture is expected to work all day today to get ready for the big event. "Just another day and another challenge for me. I am confident the rink will be frozen per league standards and ready to go for puck drop tonight," said Vulture.

Norah's Café will be selling signature berry suet cakes and hot chocolate at her food truck during the game. Jed's Pub will offer a beer garden.

Need tickets? Stop by the center box office ASAP because this game will sell out! Your Rocs will face the Trousdale Thrashing Turkeys.

Go Rocs!

Adam and I joined a large crowd at Jed's Pub for lunch. The grosbeaks were there drinking and singing Xmas carols. At one point, Elvis convinced Jed to get on the bar and sing *Santa Baby* with him. Jed had extra kegs of his Roc Bock to sell during the day and at the game that night. The merriment continued right up until game time. The birds in the bar all made their way across the town square for the game.

ROCS WIN 5-4 IN OT

FIRST OUTDOOR HOCKEY GAME A HIT

GROSBEAKS PREPARE FOR DEPARTURE

by Susan Towhee
Published December 25, 2023 in the Restful Roost Observer

It was a cold and windy night, but that didn't matter to the hundreds of fans in attendance at last night's first outdoor hockey game. Even residents of nearby Thistle Thicket and Pleasant Crest came out to see the spectacle and mingle with the visiting grosbeaks.

The rink was lit by lights hung from nearby

trees, the beer was flowing from the beer garden, snacks were sold through the event, karaoke was performed during intermissions, and good times were had by all. Except for the opposing team...

The Restful Roost Rocs won a nail-biting overtime game over the Trousdale Thrashing Turkeys. Team captain Derek Goose scored a hat trick and was involved in two fights. The final score was 5-4.

Stop by the town square at noon to wish our new feathered friends, the Evening Grosbeaks, a proper goodbye. We wish them a safe journey south and an invitation to visit again!

Merry Xmas Restful Roost!

Elvis said he and his grosbeak pals were thinking of making the trip to Restful Roost a yearly event. With a stop in Memphis as well, of course. Overall the town loved the group of birds. We all learned new facts, practiced our singing during the winter, and enjoyed a very cool hockey game! We wished the grosbeaks happy holidays and bid them farewell from the town square. Another Xmas to remember!

Just another day in Restful Roost!

~ 7 ~

WHAT REALLY HAPPENED IN 1868

ALIEN ENCOUNTERS

DETAILS ON 1868 TRAIN "EXPLOSION"

HARRY COTTONTAIL SHARES STORY

by Susan Towhee

Published January 31, 2023 in the Restful Roost Observer

Over the past year, I have been researching the events surrounding the 1868 train explosion and the October 2022 UFO visit. Both incidents occurred here in Restful Roost. Details on the train disaster were scarce and articles reporting on it were almost non-existent. It was like the event never happened and no one cared. If I had known that information provided to me by a local Cottontail rabbit (and alien abductee) would have provided all the answers I needed, I would have started my research with his story first. It turns out the train explosion didn't happen and it was all a cover-up by aliens who were determined to find answers about human and animal behaviors here on Earth.

Restful Roost residents may remember that in October 2022 a UFO landed in our town square. Harry Cottontail was on board and shared part of his story with the crowd and promised that details would follow later. This story is a follow-up to that promise. The following is a dramatized retelling of the events that occurred on November 20, 1868, as recalled by Harry Cottontail.

"It was early and I was preparing to open the gristmill my rabbit family operated near the train tracks. The mill also housed a post office and a ticket booth for train commuters. If I saw an elderly rabbit or a family in need of help, I would usually assist them with loading their luggage on board. It was on this particular day when I was helping a lady that my life changed forever.

Thunder roared and lightning crashed! I looked around and everything went dark!

When I came to, I realized I was no longer on the train. It appeared as though I was floating in the sky on some hot air balloon or something. Keep in mind, at the time, we had no concept of aircraft or the term UFO. I started walking around and realized I was on a large craft with multiple rooms. Two beings appeared that resembled what humans called "Nordic aliens" and explained to me that I was taken from a "portal" and I was now in space above the Earth. They then took me to a room that had taxidermy everywhere. I wanted to throw up because I hated seeing animal heads displayed that way. Then, the heads started talking to me! I asked the Nordics how the animals could speak. The Nordics said they did not understand their language and did not know why they were talking. The room was creepy so I asked to leave. The Nordics then took me to another room and this time the taxidermy on the walls were of human heads! Also, creepy, so I asked to leave. The Nordics then took me to another room and had me sit at a table where they asked me why the humans had been at war recently. I told them it had something to do with owning other people. The Nordics did not understand the concept of slavery. I informed them that I was a rabbit and they should ask a human to explain. Then, they took me to another room with tables and plates of food on each one. They wanted me to eat. I explained that I am a rabbit and I only like to eat grass. This confused the Nordics. My question "What do you want from me?" that I kept asking received no answers. They then said we should go to another room. I screamed that I wanted to go to no more rooms. I was starting to get angry and wanted to leave. The Nordics took me to yet another room and left me for what seemed like hours. Finally, another Nordic came in dressed like the human Pope and told me I had passed their test. I was then told the secrets of the universe and was given meditation guidance. The Nordic Pope said rabbits would be deemed the

> most holy of all creatures. I asked the Pope who our creator was and he didn't know. He said he heard that it was a guy named Kyle who had a coffee shop two planets over. At this point, I demanded to leave. Nordic Pope wiped my mind just enough for me to know that I knew important things, but not enough that I could repeat them or express them in words that others could understand. The Nordics sent me back through the portal and I remained there as a ghost since all the rabbits and other creatures alive at the time thought I died in the train "explosion." The creatures back in 1868 had their minds wiped of details. I was the only "death" that day. I was instructed to say that I was saved from the explosion if anyone ever asked about it.
>
> From time to time, the Nordics picked me up from the portal and we traveled through time and space. Nordic Pope said that later the portal would be re-opened and I could return in physical form and tell my story to the creatures that lived there now, which is what happened last year at Halloween.
>
> So, there it is. I still don't understand and I wish it hadn't happened. I guess I am immortal now? I don't know. I like to visit Restful Roost from time to time and see my family, but I live mostly in Sedona now."

Well, there it is Restful Roost! I have no extra commentary on this one folks. All I know is I needed a strong bourbon drink after that interview.

Harry Cottontail is open to questions. Send a letter to

the Old Cottontail Mill and he will answer every inquiry he gets.

Just another day in Restful Roost!

REFERENCES & INSPIRATION

Cornell Lab of Ornithology (Birdcast and All About Birds)

Michael Walters, *Birds' Eggs* (DORLING KINDERSLEY, 1994)

Jonathan Alderfer, *National Geographic Complete Birds of North America* (NATIONAL GEOGRAPHIC SOCIETY, 2014)

Hal H. Harrison, *Peterson Field Guides Eastern Birds' Nests* (HOUGHTON MIFFLIN, 1975)

S. David Scott and Casey McFarland, *Bird Feathers* (STACKPOLE BOOKS, 2010)

Phillip Hoose, *The Race to Save the Lord God Bird* (FARRAR STRAUS GIROUX, 2014)

Irby J. Lovette and John W. Fitzpatrick, *The Cornell Lab of Ornithology Handbook of Bird Biology* (Wiley, 2016)

Mark A. Michaels, Thomas C. Michot, Peggy L. Shrum, Patricia Johnson, Jay Tischendorf, Michael Weeks, John Trochet, Don Scheifler, Bob Ford, *Multiple lines of evidence suggest the persistence of the Ivory-billed Woodpecker*

(Campephilus principalis) in Louisiana (Ecology and Evolution, 2023) https://onlinelibrary.wiley.com/doi/full/10.1002/ece3.10017

Nearly 3 Billion Birds Gone
https://www.birds.cornell.edu/home/bring-birds-back/#

Steven Webb, *Learning to live with the Canada goose, a veritable 'poop machine'* (CBC, 2022)
https://www.cbc.ca/amp/1.6452349

ABOUT THE AUTHOR

Susan is an investigative reporter with the Restful Roost Observer. She is an Eastern Towhee (Pipilo erythrophthalmus) and lives with her husband, Adam, in a quaint ground nest in the community of Restful Roost, TN. Susan is a founding board member of CFRR (Cat Free Restful Roost). She also enjoys bourbon, cigars, and cozy mysteries.

Milton Keynes UK
Ingram Content Group UK Ltd.
UKHW022223050424
440549UK00004B/194

9 798218 281212